I AM NOT GUILTY

I AM NOT GUILTY

By Frances Shelley Wees

Véhicule Press

Published with the generous assistance of the Canada Council
for the Arts and the Canada Book Fund of the Department
of Canadian Heritage.

Canada Council   Conseil des arts
for the Arts   du Canada

Canada

Series editor: Brian Busby
Adaptation of original cover: J.W. Stewart
Special assistance: Willow Little and Michelle Hahn-Baker
Typeset in Minion and MrsEaves by Simon Garamond
Printed by Livres Rapido Books

LIBRARY AND ARCHIVES CANADA CATALOGUING IN PUBLICATION

Title: I am not guilty / a novel by Frances S. Wees
Other titles: M'lord, I am not guilty
Names: Wees, Frances Shelley, 1902-1982, author.
Description: Series statement: A Ricochet Book | Originally
published under title: M'lord, I am not guilty.
Garden City, N.Y. : Published for the Crime Club
by Doubleday, 1954.
Identifiers: Canadiana (print) 20200282778 |
Canadiana (ebook) 20200282786 | isbn 9781550655575
(softcover) | ISBN 9781550655612 (EPUB)
Classification: LCC PS8545. E38 M9 2020 | DDC C813/.52—dc23

Published by Véhicule Press, Montréal, Québec, Canada
www.vehiculepress.com

Distribution in Canada by LitDistCo
www.litdistco.ca

Distribution in the U.S. by Independent Publishers Group
www.ipgbook.com

Printed in Canada on FSC certified paper

To MARTHA WINSTON,
who has such infinite patience and sympathy with

"The lyf so short, the craft so long to lerne,
Th' assay so hard, so sharp the conquering."

INTRODUCTION

Patricia Abbott

I Am Not Guilty begins where many novels end: Helen Graham is found innocent of the murder of her husband, Stephen. The swift shift in her fate overwhelms Helen as she makes her way out of the Toronto courtroom. During the months spent in prison awaiting trial, Helen has realized she must solve her husband's murder if her life is not to become a prison for her and her young son. As she leaves the courthouse on her brother's arm, an onlooker confirms this by calling out, "They let her off. Get a load of that!" In the court of public opinion, her innocence remains a question mark. If Helen Graham didn't poison her husband, who did and why? Her husband was a wealthy man, he had dalliances and suspect business dealings. His family looks to profit from his death. The list of possibilities is long. Helen, as well as Toronto police consultant, Dr. Jonathan Merrill, will take different paths in ferreting out the murderer.

This novel, originally published in 1954 by Double-day, after appearing in a condensed form in *Ladies Home Journal* the same year, fits squarely into a genre that has become known as domestic suspense. Especially popular in the fifties and sixties, domestic suspense novels position the source of conflict or crime within the nuclear family. Unease permeates the home and not until the secrets and lies are laid bare is calm restored. Domestic suspense was also very much interested in psychological interpretations of familial distress. Character after character in *I Am Not Guilty*, and other novels in this genre including Wees' own *The Keys of My Prison* (1956), wrestles with misery, often placing its genesis at a mother's feet. "Women have a lot to answer for," Burke Patterson, an artist in Mapleton, the setting of much of this novel, pronounces. With few exceptions, mothers in domestic suspense novels have been driven back into the kitchen or bedroom by the evolving trends of a post-war society that no longer requires their services in the workplace.

For these post-war women, finding agency is difficult. Helen Graham has been beaten down by her husband over their decade of marriage. Newly wealthy from Alberta oil deals, Stephen Graham was dissatisfied with Helen's wardrobe and had wanted her to spend hours at beauty spas. He'd instructed her in the matter of food, imposing his judgment, his selection, on everything in their life. He was bolstered in his Pygmalion endeavor by the magazines of the day where stories, articles, and even advertisements tell women their place is in the home.

Female novelists in the United States, such as Elisabeth Sanxay Holding, Dorothy B. Hughes, and Charlotte Armstrong, shaped their suspense novels to reflect the new post-war reality. Gone are the *femmes fatales* of novels of the forties—in their place are fifties women who are expected to find satisfaction in their new wall oven, in a suburban home in a hurriedly constructed sub-division. In Canada, Margaret Millar, perhaps the greatest practitioner of this genre, and Frances Shelley Wees wrote dozens of suspense books reflecting, if not condoning, these new values. In Australia, Charlotte Jay received the inaugural Edgar Best Novel Award for *Beat Not the Bones* (1952), which features a story somewhat similar to *I Am Not Guilty*. Here a widow is forced into detective work when her husband's death is wrongly called suicide.

Domestic references abound in *I Am Not Guilty*. There is an early mention of the contrast between home-spun fabric (honest, useful) to satin (only for looks). The novel is peopled with gardeners, housekeepers, and seamstresses. Such domesticity would have been performed off-stage ten years earlier (or later) if set in an urbane city like Toronto, but it now takes centre stage in small-town Mapleton. Also portrayed is the country club set and those who do for them, Wees describing their drink, their homes, their dress, their leisure activities.

"We do everything out there, from little theater to lawn bowling," Burke says of life at the Country Club. Through well-placed agents, much is discovered through the overheard gossip of women, and by the overheated remarks of men.

So along with a tidy and well-plotted mystery, *I Am Not Guilty* is a document of cultural history, telling us much about how Canadians lived a decade after the war. Ten years later, great change would again occur as women demanded to play an equal part in public life. And the domestic novel would recede for a generation.

PATRICIA ABBOTT is the author of the mystery novels *Concrete Angel* (2015) and the Edgar Award-nominated *Shot in Detroit* (2016). Her collection *I Bring Sorrow and Other Stories* was published in 2018.

ONE

She stood in her high-railed prisoner's box as the plump affable judge concluded his neatly tailored remarks. Later she would recall his words and think them over; her mind was housewifely, and always tucked odds and ends away carefully for future use. Now, all her ears could accept was the conclusion of the jury…We find her not guilty. We find her not guilty. She was free.

In the four months of her imprisonment Helen had faced the other possible verdict. She had deliberately looked at the noose—the awful rope—but she had never, never believed in its reality. Never. Her certainty had kept her calm, kept her voice serene, her manner unafraid; her very fearlessness, her openness, influenced the jury mightily, her lawyer said. There was not one trace of guilt anywhere about her.

It had been difficult to get a jury together, since this case had been such a newspaper and radio sensation. And it was the sort of case, Mr. Pentford had explained worriedly, that seems settled before it is tried. A young man, found mysteriously dead in his own apartment, a man with a great deal of money, all of which his attractive wife inherits, no one else with motive—even if the death looks like suicide or accident it is practically a foregone conclusion in the public mind that the wife is the killer. Everyone knows how many marital quarrels are hidden.

The happiest-appearing marriages may be miserable torture. Many of the people who had been summoned for jury duty had already decided that Helen must be guilty. The twelve who were finally assembled were an odd lot, socially incongruous; not the sort of jury whose conclusions one could predict.

One middle-aged spinster was obviously the core of the assemblage. Middle-aged spinsters could be dangerous. The foreman was a frustrated-looking person, a plumber by trade; he had delivered the verdict with a sweaty face and a dank lock of hair dangling over his eye, and he was seriously unhappy at this critical job of weighing the bloody guilt of a young and wealthy woman. He had muttered in a barely audible voice, "We find the prisoner not guilty," and sat down with limp relief to mop his forehead.

The prim spinster beside him nodded in strong approval of his words, so that she had, after all, been no enemy. It looked as if she might be the person who all along had directed the jury's thinking, and if that were true, it was something like being touched by the finger of God.

The judge's round pink cheeks bobbed as he finished his remarks about the ease with which the innocent can be confused with the guilty, when they carelessly allow themselves to become involved with murder. What he said didn't matter. What was important was that he called Helen again by her name. She was no longer "Prisoner at the bar," she was Mrs. Graham, and was free to go.

The tall policeman who had been her special guard stepped forward and opened the latched gate of the box. He had called for her each morning at the Don jail, to escort her into the Black Maria and sit with her as they rode to the City Hall; he had taken her back each evening. Helen walked through the gate he held open for her and down the steps to the aisle, holding her eyes steady and her mouth serene to meet the avid upturned stares of the crowded courtroom.

At the back of the room a man rose, and for a moment their eyes met. His were clear and calm, thoughtful eyes, big and luminous, set in a thin long face surmounted by an unruly thatch of reddish hair. This was Jonathan Merrill, Dr. Jonathan Merrill, psychological consultant to the Toronto police, who had come once to the Don jail to interview her, back at the beginning of her imprisonment. He had a gentle manner and a quiet, almost hesitant way of questioning, as if the questions in words did not matter; as if those eyes saw through to the truth. He was leaving the courtroom now; he gave her a nod, almost imperceptible, and melted through the crowd at the back of the room.

As Helen reached the lowest step, Jerry, her brother, stood up from his chair at the end of the fourth row, and moved toward her. His thin young face was terribly changed. His eyes brooded, dark and shuttered. There were deep lines at the corners of his tightly pressed mouth. He took her arm quickly and moved her down the aisle. Behind them were judge, jury, the tall policeman, and the lawyers...her own lawyer, quiet, honest, determined, and the prosecuting attorney, whose every word, every question, every suggestion had made it seem that it mattered to him personally that Steven was dead, that the death was tragic, monstrous, and that he was bent on revenge, not justice. He had lost his case. He would be angry.

The people in the audience were not happy, either. There was no Christian left for the lions to devour, and lions were always hungry. Their faces were dubious, unsatisfied. A man was murdered, an interesting, dramatic, wealthy young Canadian with a long Toronto family history. There was more going on in these families than anybody knew. These people weren't any better than the man in the street, you came to look into it. But this girl was going free after all. In spite of the evidence, she was going free.

Who *had* killed Steven Graham? How had he really died?

Jerry's fingers tightened on her arm. Halfway down the aisle a heavy-set reporter with black eyebrows got to his feet, but Jerry put a savage hand on his shoulder and pushed him down again. They reached the grimy wide door of the courtroom, and the old man standing there on guard peered at Helen nearsightedly as if he had been trying all through the proceedings to see what she really looked like. He had pale rheumy eyes and tobacco-stained snagged teeth. There was a dribble of ashes down the front of his coat, a sagging blue garment which looked like the uniform of a train conductor with the shiny buttons removed, and very likely was.

Jerry said bitterly, "Open the door, will you?"

The old man stared at him, but turned the brass knob without speaking. The door swung open. The sounds of the world outside, the polyglot mutter of the City Hall, were like a warm thick wave breaking. The door opened outward, and with difficulty; the old man stepped forward, put his head into the wide gloomy corridor, and said irritably, "Get back, you! Don't jam this here door shut! How many times a day I got to tell you?"

A crowd of youngsters waited in the corridor, teen-age girls in bobby socks and bright sweaters, lanky pimply schoolboys with hands thrust into trouser pockets. They fixed their eyes on Helen and Jerry. One small rounded blonde looked at Jerry again and gave a smart imitation of a wolf whistle.

Someone said loudly, "Gee! They let her off! Get a load of that!"

"Then who did it? Who *did* it? Hey… Mrs. Helen Graham, who did it?"

Jerry said, "Get out of the way, for God's sake! Go home and mind your own bloody business, damn you!"

Helen said under her breath, "Jerry, Jerry." She put her hand quickly over his. They walked swiftly along to the head of the wide staircase and down the shallow dirty steps, littered with scraps of paper and grimy with dust. They were suddenly out in the sunlight, not walking through the inner quadrangle at whose door the Black Maria had discharged her each day, but out on the open pavement of Bay Street. The curious youngsters clattered down the stairs behind them, but Jerry swung her across on the changing traffic light, and a line of automobiles and a streetcar cut off most of the pursuers. They moved along Albert to the parking lot and Jerry hurried her through it. He said, "I brought Dad's car. I thought my jalopy was too informal. His voice was rough.

The familiar black Pontiac, a little shabby and never well polished, sat at the edge of the lot. The attendant waved a casual hand. Jerry slid Helen into the front seat, went round and climbed in under the wheel. Four or five of the gaping youngsters from the City Hall came racing through the parking lot. Jerry jerked the car forward, into the narrow lane and out to the street. His driving had always been impulsive; now it was apparently unaware of the bounds of time, space, traffic lights, or the congestion of busses and trucks in narrow Albert Street. He tore around the curve toward the armories and then came out on University Avenue, broad and less dangerous. He turned north. They passed the sprawling buildings of the hospitals, crossed College, swung around the circle of Queen's Park, went up to Bloor. Above it, he turned off into a side street and stopped the car. He sat for half a minute silent, then dropped his dark curly head into his long hands and said under his breath, "Oh, God, I've been so scared. Oh, God, I've been so scared."

"I know, darling."

He lifted his head and looked at her. Tears glittered in his eyes.

"I got to thinking...an eye for an eye, a tooth for a tooth...it seemed to me that everybody in that rotten place has been thinking it too, and not really caring whose eye or whose tooth...They had their clutches on you and they didn't intend to let you go. Talk about British justice! Talk about being innocent until you are proven guilty..." He stopped, and sat looking at her, his eyes taking in the planes of her face, searching her expression. "You were wonderful," he said huskily. "Was there anything they didn't do to try to pin that damned thing on you? Anything?"

"They didn't succeed."

"That last while, when the jury was out, I thought I'd go crazy. If only they'd have let me go back and be with you...but you were all alone. It's damnable, that's what it is! To throw you in prison, when you've just found your husband dead...leave you there alone, only seeing one or two of us, a few minutes at a time...alone, no bail. Four months! My God, haven't they got any mercy? Four months, locked up like an animal..."

"It's all over, Jerry."

"How can you be so calm? You're not really calm. It's—you're—it's as if you've been locked in a deep freeze." He took her hand roughly and held it in a close grip. "It isn't only the trial, either. I've come to see that. You started this ice business years ago. It's got something to do with Steve. Thank God for that. I mean, all the time...I was thinking, 'Thank God, she won't be grieving over Steve's being dead.' It was the only comfort I had. Mom knew it too. She kept telling Dad."

"What are they doing for her, Jerry? How is she?"

"She'll be all right now. Doc Innis had been giving her lots of sedative lately, though. It's the strain, just waiting, not knowing. The papers...they'd come out with a case against you, it looked black as hell. Next day they'd ease off. But that letter—and the money—and the stuff he died of—those stories nearly killed Mom and Dad. Dad's hands have been shaking; he hasn't been able to hold a glass of water for days. But it'll be all right now. I had Tod Hawkins primed to dash out and telephone the minute the verdict came down, before that old windbag started making his speech. So they know. You want to go out there?"

"I want to go to the apartment first."

"You can't do that."

"Yes, I can. They put the keys back into my purse."

"You can't go back there now. Give yourself a break! Come on out home…have a couple of stiff drinks…let old Doc Innis look you over—maybe you ought to have some kind of treatment, I don't know. You don't seem natural to me. You can't go back to the apartment."

"There's nothing wrong with me. I'm calm and collected because I've had so much time to think. I *can* go back to the apartment. I must. Then I'll go home with you for tonight and see Mother and Dad. I didn't kill Steve. I told them so, and now they've had to agree. In words, anyway," she heard herself say briefly. "And it's no use trying to run away. I want to go back as soon as possible and get started…"

"Get started at what?"

"Oh," she said quickly, "get started at a new life. There's Jamie to think of. He hasn't seen me for months. There'll soon be holidays coming. Thank God, he's really seen very little of Steven. And he's only six. Oh, I'm so glad he's been at school! I'm so glad I sent him there to board last fall!"

"Helen…"

"Yes?"

"What did you know last fall?"

"Nothing. There was nothing to know."

17

"I think you're lying. I've thought all along—" He stopped. "What are you going to do now?"

"I'm not sure. I don't know exactly." She smiled at him. "It's never any good putting off facing things," she reminded him. "Take me to the apartment, Jerry. Take me home."

"Home!" he repeated angrily. But he let in the clutch with a kind of relief. The responsibility was off his shoulders. He was young; twenty-three was very young.

TWO

Matthew Graham, driving the Buick limousine with his mother as his passenger, was later in getting away from the City Hall courtroom and the trial of his brother's widow for his brother's murder. His mother, erect and white-faced, had not moved since the verdict was given. She was quite aware of the emptying courtroom, of the curious stares directed upon her. She sat with her eyes fixed upon the judge until he left the room by the door at the back; and then she stared at the wall, refusing to acknowledge the presence of the prosecutor, who at one uneasy point looked as if he might be coming down to speak to them. There wasn't much left for the fellow to say. He had said it. He had taken every shred of the evidence, particularly the letter from Steven to his mother, and made the most of it. He had done his best to pin the murder on the girl, and he had failed. That was it.

After two or three half glances in their direction he had gathered up his papers and left, with his three or four younger satellites. After all, Matthew sat thinking to himself, it wouldn't do to create any impression that he had been working for them, the Grahams; that he had been anxious for their sake to prove the girl guilty. This was supposed to be a court of impartial justice.

The room was empty. His mother stirred. She gathered her black Persian lamb coat about her, took her velvet bag firmly into her grasp, and rose. "Come, Matthew," she said.

There were reporters at the door, hovering. Mrs. Graham's face was stony. Matthew hesitated briefly. He said in a low voice, "We have nothing to say," and followed his mother's uncompromising figure along the outer corridor. They went downstairs, out to the street, along to the parking lot, and got into the car in silence.

His mother laid her black veil carefully back over the brim of her small black hat. The four months since Steven's death had lined her face savagely, darkened the skin, left her haggard and drained of life.

She had, after all, pinned all her hopes on Steven.

Matthew turned north. It was late April, and ahead the spreading ancient trees of Rosedale were green with tender new leaf.

"Where did she go, Matthew?"

"Helen?"

"Who else?"

"Her brother took her away. Probably they went out to her family's. To Parkdale. The mother has had a sort of stroke."

"So where is the father?"

"He's rather broken up too. They've had a bad time."

"And what would you say has happened to me? My son…my son…my handsome, successful boy…dead, at the very opening of his life, at the very beginning of his success…"

Matthew rubbed a finger carefully along his cheek. But he said calmly enough, "Don't let yourself go, Mother. We mustn't have you cracking up too."

The car slid along the street, turned in at their own drive, came to a halt under the old-fashioned but still impressive port cochere. The Grahams had built this ugly red brick mansion three generations ago, when the money from whiskey stocks and railroad bonds and ship holdings was still flowing like water, before Matthew's father had got his loose fingers into the glittering stream. Loose fingers, a loose mind, a roving eye…and a wife with a rigid standard and a bitter tongue.

They sat for a moment when the care had stopped. His mother looked up at him. Her eyelids had developed an odd triangularity, as if the middle were held up by a small picture nail, but with the outside edges drooping like old dingy wet flannel. Inside the triangle her eyes were, these days, abnormally bright. She said, "We cannot possibly let her keep the money."

Matthew unfastened his door and got out. He went around and helped her down to the cement step in the drive. She moved as if she were eighty; as if her bones felt brittle and in imminent danger of breaking.

They went in through the wide side door and up the four steps to the hall. Jane, the new maid, came from the back hall as they reached the step. Her face was blank, her manner perfect. She was extremely superior for a maid.

"A cup of tea," Mrs. Graham said harshly. "In the library."

Matthew followed his mother along the hall. He stopped before the hall mirror and smoothed down his hair. It was beginning to thin, but it was still black and with a certain waviness that hid the thinning. He looked well these days, he decided. He'd had to lead a pretty circumspect life all through the late weeks and particularly through these days of the trial. Likely a week or so of such rigid living would be good for him, every now and then. The muscles of his face were tightened up and his eyes were clear and steady.

He took his mother's coat. It was a nice thing, one of Steven's first presents after he had hit the jackpot, five years ago. Not mink; because Steven had a streak of sadism in him and he enjoyed showing that he had control. What his mother had wanted, of course, was everything all at once...a Cadillac instead of a Buick, mink instead of lamb, a houseful of servants, and all Steve's money in her bank account. Nothing less would repair the old cruel damage done by his father to her soul. But Steve wouldn't do things her way...not always. And Steve had held the reins.

There was a small brisk fire burning on the hearth. She went across and sat down in her own chair, a chair with a high seat and a straight back done in gray needlepoint. Matthew bent to the fire, gave it a needless poke, and then said carefully, "I think I'll change my coat."

She did not look up from her contemplation of the fire. Her mind was far away. Matthew went out of the room unobtrusively and shut the door behind him. In the hall he turned and went upstairs sedately enough, but the thought of the drink that was so assuredly coming to him, so well earned, began to nibble at him; so that by the time he got into his own room, with the door shut and bolted, with the bottom drawer of his desk unlocked and the dark bottle of rye in his hand, he was shaking. He could scarcely get the top unscrewed from the bottle. He poured himself three fingers, fastened the bottle, slid it back into the drawer. In half a minute the warmth began to course through his veins. He dropped down on the foot of his bed while the magic worked. Soon he began to feel like a man, someone with guts and fire, not afraid of anything, sure of himself and his rights. He would have liked to stay right here and keep on feeling wonderful; but his mother wouldn't wait too long for his return. She would send for him.

He glanced at the bolt on the door, got up, got out the bottle, regarded it thoughtfully. It was only half full. He'd have to get to the vendor before six o'clock somehow. Probably he shouldn't take any more right now. But he needed it. The rest of the day was going to be tough, full of problems. He couldn't get anywhere with them unless he had some courage, unless the empty places in him were covered over. He took only two fingers, however, and then hastily pushed the bottle into the drawer and went out of the room before he could talk himself into another small nip. A half bottle wasn't much, and it had to tide him over until he could get out to buy more.

THREE

Jane stood at the counter in the narrow butler's pantry and arranged the tea tray carefully. Mrs. Graham was particular about such important matters as the arrangement of tea trays, and this was the best tray. It was a massive thing, and old. Silver fishes twined together to form the handles and there was a design of fine chasing on the flat bottom. It was supposed to be a family piece; but upon occasion when Mr. Matthew Graham had taken six or seven drinks over the Plimsoll line, he had divulged proudly that he had found it in a junk shop, black as coal, and bought it for three dollars. It had taken a great deal of cleaning to get it looking like anything, he had explained, but now that it was in shape it did as well as, maybe better than, Sheffield. It had guts, that tray, Matthew said. It was the real thing. Matthew respected guts. He liked the word.

The white Wedgwood with the powder-blue grapes along the edge seemed indicated at the moment. That china, a few cups and tea plates and a large soup tureen left of a set, really had been in the family for a while, and the sight of it always seemed to act on Mrs. Graham as if you'd given her a thrust in the vertebrae with a sharp thumb. Jane set two of the Wedgwood cups on the tray beside the silver teapot and hot-water jug, laid out the spoons, filled the jug with milk—cream was not the thing—and made sure that the sugar bowl was full. She glanced at the clock. It was only three, so that a proper tea would not be regarded with favor. However, she got a few thin ginger cookies from the jar on the top shelf and put them on a plate. The lady of the house was looking gaunt these days, what with one thing and another, and eating practically nothing.

She carried the tray to the library.

Mrs. Graham sat staring into the fire. She was down to about ninety pounds, and if there had been any threads of gold in the silver of her hair four months ago, they were gone now. She had once been a beautiful woman. Her portrait hung above the mantle now, over the fire. She had been a true golden blonde, with masses of hair piled on her head and coiled to cover her ears. Jane gave the picture a quick glace. The two boys were in the picture, Matthew a lad of twelve or so, standing tall and manly with a hand on his mother's shoulder, and Steven a three-year-old sitting on her knee.

She drew up the small table to set it beside Mrs. Graham's chair and put the tea tray on it. The woman looked half dead, her thin hands motionless in her lap, her eyes fixed on the fire.

"Shall I pour for you, madam?"

"Certainly not." She stirred. "Where is Mr. Matthew?"

"I will remind him, madam."

Mrs. Graham reached out and poured herself a cup of the tea. It was properly boiling hot, the tray was perfect. Her eyes went over everything. The ginger cookies got by. As her eyes encountered them she said, "I omitted speaking this morning to Cook. There is cold lamb, is there not?"

"Yes, madam."

"Tell Cook there will be three at table."

"Would you perhaps care for a curry, madam? Cook is very good with curries."

Mrs. Graham shot her a swift, knowing glance. She

knows there isn't enough lamb, Jane thought. She knows to a hair how much there is of everything. She never misses a thing. So…she doesn't know that our Matthew is half sozzled all the time? Doesn't know? Or…doesn't care, as long as other people don't know?

"Yes, curry," she said. Then, "Kindly remind Mr. Matthew that tea is ready."

He came in as she spoke. His eyes were a little brighter, and there was a hint of color in his cheeks. But he carried his liquor well. He could get by with anything under a gallon. "Sorry," he said. "I can do with a cup of tea too. It's a raw day."

His mother poured the tea in silence. Jane stood behind the corner of the old lady's chair. Mrs. Graham handed Matthew his cup. She said, "When you've drunk it, go and telephone the Brown house. Helen will be there, I expect. When you get her, invite her to dinner."

"Tonight?"

"Certainly, tonight."

He sipped at his tea. He looked as if he were about to protest. Then some thought went across his mind. "Shall I suggest going to get her? Her car's in storage."

"Unless she went directly to the garage," his mother said acidly, "which she well might have done. It's a beautiful car, as I remember."

"I'd think she'd go right home with her brother. I'll go for her."

"There are taxicabs."

"She isn't going to be too fond of public appearances."

"Well, offer to go for her if you like. But get her here, that's what matters."

"And if she refuses to come?"

"Tell her she *must* come." She straightened her back. "I will not take no for an answer. This situation is intolerable."

FOUR

Helen's penthouse was in one of the new buildings on Eglinton. The garage was in the basement. A double stall had been reserved there for Steven Graham and his wife, with room for Steven's long mustard-colored Cadillac and Helen's dark blue Packard coupé. The police had stored the cars elsewhere for safety; Jerry slid the small Pontiac into the reserved area.

Helen walked slowly toward the door at the inner end of the basement, the door opening into the elevator foyer. She was getting her keys from her bag. Watching her slender figure, her slow graceful walk, remembering the serenity of her face all through the trial, even today when he himself had felt like bawling openly, Jerry's mind was filled again with wonder and admiration.

The small square hallway held no doors except that of the elevator. The red light showed that the lift was stationary on the third floor. Jerry put out a thumb and summoned it. He thought again, as he had so many times, how simple it would have been for anyone to get up to that penthouse on the night of Steve's death. If you had no keys, you could get in through the tradesmen's door, which was open from seven in the morning until eleven at night.

The elevator came down. Its door held no glass. Once inside it, you were invisible, and if you kept your thumb on the button nobody could stop the thing until you were safely out of it.

Keys could be stolen, copied.

But there was nothing to suggest that any stranger had been with Steven the night he died. Nothing. He had been alone. His death hadn't looked like murder. It had looked like suicide, except—well, as Steven's mother had put it with such force and anger, why would Steven have wanted to kill himself? He'd only had his big, lush, marvelous oil money for five years. He'd only begun to enjoy it. He was young, handsome, strong, brave, beautiful, magnificent, generous, noble, sweet-tempered, with gourmet tastes and a delightful sense of humor and a forward look in his big beautiful godlike mind, according to his mother. There was enough superficial truth in what she said to make a little sense, even when you knew the guy was a heel. Anyway, he was a coward. He wouldn't have had the nerve to kill himself, even if he'd wanted to.

Accident? It must have been an accident.

No suicide; no villainous stranger. Not Helen, in spite of the damning letter Steven had written about her to his mother, and the other fifty-seven details the police had dug up. They'd all fallen to ashes under the truth Pentford had brought out. So…accident.

"But my son was meticulous," his mother had said. "He was famous for his meticulous habits. He would *never* accidentally have taken an overdose of sedative. Never."

Helen took a long unconscious breath as the elevator rose, and Jerry rested his eyes on her. Her own were deep and lost, far away in some hidden thought. They were beautiful eyes; maybe the only beautiful thing about her, big and gray, with a thick fringe of black lashes edging the underlid, sort of remarkable. You didn't forget them. The rest of her was probably ordinary enough to other people—dark brown hair, not slick and shining, but just soft around her face and pulled back into a thick knot at the back of her head. It was parted in the middle. Her mouth was nice, but it was changed. When she was younger, before these last years with Steve, it had been soft and with a look as if it might smile any second. Now it was firm and steady, and there was no laughter anywhere in her.

The car stopped. The door slid open noiselessly. Jerry stepped out to the thickly carpeted hall and held a hand back for Helen. She took it. They moved forward to the only door on this top floor, the wide pale gray door directly opposite. Helen dropped his hand, lifted her key ring, and slid her key into the lock.

Inside, the small oblong foyer was very smart. The place had been done to Steven's taste. This floor was of black and white squares and the walls were covered with mirrors. Steven had liked lots of mirrors. He'd been tall and wide, with very white skin and very black hair and long hazel eyes that were lazy and tilted at the corners. Jerry thought suddenly, "Young Jamie has his father's eyes. Maybe that's a worry to Helen…young Jamie with his father's eyes."

She opened that door into the living room, the door through which she'd come on the night of Steven's death.

Jerry said gruffly, "You want I should open a few windows?"

"I don't suppose it's been aired…"

"You were in that damned jail for nearly four months. I don't doubt they took the place apart and put it together again, looking for a signed confession from you, or some damned thing." He went across the room to the sweep of plate glass on the south, overlooking the city. There were some capable catches to turn; the panels of glass swung lightly open and the fresh damp April air poured gratefully into the dead atmosphere of the room. They were far above the city here; the treetops of Forest Hill Village, misty and pale as green lace, lay like a veil over the houses.

"Jerry, you are swearing dreadfully."

He turned and grinned at her. "Am I? Sorry."

"You never used to."

"My morals are all shot to hell. I've lost all respect for everything." He twisted the last catch. "I wouldn't have thought it could happen to a dog, what they did to you.

I thought—well, the police would try to save you, a girl with a name and a reputation as sound and decent as yours. They didn't. They tried to throw you to the dogs. I thought—maybe I thought the Church would step in. I though *something* would happen. My God, they can't do this kind of thing to decent people! They didn't treat you a bit better than a common criminal. A filthy barred cell in a jail, that damned rattling hearse they carry common drunks in, the—"

"Be quiet!"

He met her eyes. After a long moment he said gently, "Okay. If that's the way you want it."

She turned. She looked deliberately at the low wide couch piled with cushions, the couch upon which she had found Steven's body. She had thought him sleeping, she had said, lying there in his pajamas and the dressing gown of dark gold satin. He had looked very peaceful, relaxed.

There had been no glass on the small end table. Steven had died from a staggering draught of his own brand of sleeping medicine...but there had been no glass.

Helen walked over and sat down in the armchair at the end of the couch. She moved slowly. Jerry realized what she was doing. She was dipping her hand in hot water after it had been badly burned. She was holding it there. He had seen her do it in actuality when she was younger. It had always been her remedy.

"Helen?"

"Mhm?"

"Did you love the guy?"

She said slowly, "I don't think I know. I was sure I did, when I married him. But I was young and romantic...unrealistic. I'd never known anyone like Steven, handsome, beautifully mannered, attentive in all the courting ways, and—well, we all thought he was wealthy, didn't we? Not that I cared about that, except that he was like Prince Charming come true, and he wanted me. He wanted me very much." She stopped. "What is love? He wasn't a good person. I am not going to let Jamie grow up to be like him."

"I hated him."

"You liked him when I married him."

"He had a way about him."

"He had great charm," she said thoughtfully.

"I think he was a devil, if you want my thinking. I don't think he had any heart or any soul. After he got his money—after his peach twig brought up that oil in Alberta, or whatever *did* get it for him—he seemed to uncover. He peeled off the shiny layers. You know what?" Jerry squinted at the smoke curling into the damp air. "He used to scare me. As if—if he went far enough—hidden inside somewhere…"

She looked up at him again, and he stopped. Well, he'd said it.

After a while she said slowly, "He hadn't much chance to develop goodness and strength, Jerry."

"His mother?"

She nodded.

She ought to know. When she'd married Steve they'd had to go to live—in spite of all Steve's bright half plans—with old Mrs. Graham and Matthew. At that time most people thought the Grahams had money. Some had even hinted that Helen had married Steven for his money. But there hadn't been any. The big house in Rosedale hadn't been much better than a glorified boardinghouse, although nobody would ever call it that. It held three or four small suites, rented for high rates, and a few people even took their meals at the Graham table. In those days Matthew had worked occasionally, always in some fly-by-night promotion scheme where his old family contacts meant a good deal, and Steven had always had some sort of job. Steven could sell anything. But he hated having bosses. He couldn't stand them. What it all amounted to was that Helen had had to be a sort of servant in the Graham house—Mrs. Graham saw to that.

Jerry's eyes roved over the shadowy room, gray and crimson, over the grand piano in the alcove, the elegant custom-built television set in its niche, the thick soft rug, the paintings on the walls. He looked at Helen, slender and neat in her black dress, at her long slim hands that had always liked to work around the cookstove of their cottage up on Echo Lake, or paddle a canoe, or help carry stones for damns on the brook. He said, "How much money is there actually? The figure seemed to change according to the side testifying."

The question fell into the quiet of the room. Helen took a deep breath. "About half a million dollars."

"Oh *no*!"

She regarded him thoughtfully. "They had *reason* to think he wouldn't have killed himself."

"Were you telling the truth when you said you had no idea it was all left to you?"

"I told nothing but the truth whenever I was questioned, Jerry."

She didn't say, "I told *all* the truth."

"You didn't know how much there was?"

"I didn't even guess. I don't think Steven knew himself, it had skyrocketed and increased so fast. And the will was made when we were first married. He had nothing to leave me then, not a dollar. I kept it only as a memento of a happy time…" She stopped. "He hadn't got around to thinking about wills again. It was the only one he'd ever made. If he'd intended to kill himself…"

"He wouldn't have left everything to you? No, I suppose not." He thought that over. "What are you going to do with the money?"

"You want some?"

"No, I don't want Steve Graham's wildcat money and, what's more, I don't imagine you do either. Do you?"

"I want every penny of it."

He stared at her.

"It might take half a million dollars to make a decent life for Jamie and give him a chance to be a man, free of all this history."

Jerry got up. He walked to the window and looked out. He said, "To be free of any history you have to clear up all the dark hidden bits, don't you?"

She said nothing.

"Helen…how do you think Steven died?"

She moved in her chair. She said, "I could have killed him. If I'd been the prosecuting attorney I'd have made out a stronger case against the prisoner."

"How could you have killed him? He died of the sleeping stuff. It had to be self-administered. You couldn't hold a man and pour it down him. He must have taken it himself. I know it's confusing. But he *must* have taken it himself. How could you have killed him?"

Her eyes were clear. "Lots of people will still think I could, and they are justified. I'm just unbelievably lucky that I put the investigating of the money, and my responsibility on signing papers for Steven, into Mr. Pentford's hands a way before Christmas. So that he understood that letter and had all the facts in hand."

"Steven didn't know you'd gone to the lawyer?"

"He didn't dream of my being so determined. He didn't realize that I'd come to the end of one kind of life and wasn't going on another minute on a base of dishonesty, maybe even on money that was stolen."

"There wasn't any tangle about that, then, that didn't come out?"

"Nothing."

"But you might have had some other motive for

killing him?"

"I'm saying…as for *method*, I could have done it. Very easily."

"How?"

"I could have been storing up a supply of his sleeping stuff. He always had two or three bottles—in a briefcase, a suitcase, the medicine cabinet. Steven was awfully dependent on that drug. He was afraid to go anywhere without it. He was terrified at the thought of not sleeping. And if he'd been drinking heavily he never could sleep. He often took small doses in the daytime, to relax his nerves. Often. That night…he'd changed into pajamas as if he were going to bed…but it was too early. I think he'd planned a nap before…"

"Before what?"

"Probably before going out again."

Her face had no expression. Jerry said, "So how could you have got him to take a lethal dose?"

"By putting it into another drink. It would have been terribly simple."

"You weren't here. You weren't pouring his drinks that night, thank God."

"No…but I might have mixed him a shaker of cocktails and left it in the refrigerator. He would have been pleased if I'd done that and left him a note to say it was there. If I'd done that he'd have seen it as giving up my stiff-necked prudishness, as he called it. I didn't know he was coming home; that's why I went down to Mother's, as you know. But if I *had* known I could have left a mixed drink and a note for him."

"And he'd have come in…planning to bathe, dress, and go out later," Jerry said slowly, "and taken his drink. But there's the amount, Helen. A whole shaker full—the stuff would be diluted. By the time he'd drunk it all…it would take too long. Unless…when you came in…you *did* wash his glass, the shaker."

"They were Steven's fingerprints on the glass in the

medicine cabinet, not mine; and mine weren't on the *empty* pentobarb bottle, only Steven's."

"You don't think he took enough from there to kill him?"

"There wasn't so much left in that bottle, Jerry. I know. There wasn't more than a good tablespoonful. I think he took that, yes; but it wasn't enough. I didn't tell how much was in the bottle. I said I didn't know. I don't, not to swear to it. But after years of watching I'm pretty sure. There wasn't enough in that bottle, and the new one hadn't been opened. Somewhere else he had had more, enough to make up a lethal amount. And I *could* have given it. Maybe I needn't have made up a whole shaker full of drinks—just one well-flavored drink, in a frosted glass."

"And the glass?"

"That's so simple. A hundred times I've seen him carry his glass to the tap and wash it, almost before the drink was finished. It was a kind of compulsion. There'd be a mouthful left…he'd get up, saying maybe he'd have another…and if he had one, of course he'd just fill the glass. But if he'd had enough he'd drink down the last drops, wash the glass, and put it away. All the time they were talking about the glass I wanted to say what a fuss about nothing…because of that trick of Steven's. I'm sure that's what happened—if he really had the big dose here at home. And I don't see how he could have had it elsewhere and then driven the car home. The bit he took in the bathroom—when he left his fresh clear prints on the glass and the bottle—that only finished the job. Surely it did."

"You mean," Jerry said slowly, "you really think he was murdered?"

"I haven't said that. I'm just…thinking out loud. I said, I could have killed him. I didn't. But I could have."

"Someone else may have been here, Helen. Somebody who had Steve's confidence."

"There was no trace of the visit of anyone else. I've gone over it and over it."

He walked across the floor and back. He said, "Do you know anyone in the world who had a motive to kill him? Are you keeping something back? Do you know anyone who might have killed him? Is that what you're turning over in your mind? Are you...thinking you might track down the killer yourself? Are you?"

She got up. She said evenly, "If the police got only as far as me in four months, Jerry, where do you think my simple procedures would get, even if I had anything to go on?"

FIVE

Helen, the next morning, sat on the edge of the wide satin-covered bed which had been Steven's and hers. Her hand lay on the glassy surface of the heavy satin and her mind considered it absently. Before she married, the plaid bedspread in her room in the old house in Parkdale had been made of loosely woven homespun, a perfect material for the purpose. All the Browns were great readers, much given to leaving books propped open everywhere, and to dropping down on any convenient surface to read. Beds were singularly adapted for long hours of reading; you lay on your stomach for a while, propped on your elbows, and when your arms got numb you turned over and lay on your back, holding the book over your head for a few minutes to read that way. Or stacked pillows against the headboard and sat there, eating apples and making your way through everything from *Clarissa Harlowe* (Lit. 2D required reading) down through *The Old Wives' Tale*, *Main Street*, and *The Grapes of Wrath*. Homespun was an honest, useful material. It could be popped into the tub every week, if necessary, and it never needed ironing. This stuff, this pale sleek demanding satin, was only for looks. A bed was a bed, and that was that.

Steven was dead.

She had not killed him.

He had never, never killed himself.

His death was no accident. He had been taking his elixir pentobarb for years; he didn't like it in capsules as most people took it, because you couldn't gauge the exact dosage you needed. He knew exactly to a drop what it would do for him. He had tried all the other sedatives and they were not good, but this clear liquid seemed to supply something his physical system craved. He *would* have gone into the bathroom, here off the bedroom, he had done that, and poured himself out a careful dose; under the circumstances, probably two teaspoonfuls, since that was what he usually took when he wanted a daytime or evening nap, preparing for later revels of some sort or another. He would not have taken more... perhaps a very few drops extra, but no more. He had planned to go out at least for the evening. He said, "I may be away all week end." He hadn't said exactly where he'd be. But sometimes he went out of town, or said he did. Sometimes he got into drinking parties and stayed wherever he was, with his men friends at the hotel, at their clubs. Sometimes he slept at his mother's, if he were downtown and didn't relish the thought of driving all the way home.

He'd known she was going to be out; she had said she'd go home to see her own people. He would have expected the apartment to be empty. So he had come home to change his clothes...hadn't he? Not to go to bed. Steven never went to bed before the small hours of the morning. Never. Let the police think what they liked. She knew better.

What did the police think? Had they given up the

case? They had been so persistent, so diligent at pursuing every possible lead that might further incriminate her. Now that she was exonerated, legally at any rate, were they content? Was this the end of justice?

She got up from the bed and went to look at herself in the mirror. She was too thin. The black dress made the thinness very obvious. She unfastened it at the neck and took it off, to put it away in the cupboard and then to stand looking at the clothes hanging there. She had never pleased Steven with her wardrobe—her tastes were unformed, he said, she had no feeling for elegance, no interest in style. He had wanted her to show off his money, to have a wardrobe like that of a movie star, to appear in a different costume on every new occasion. One day she was to wear the mink coat he had bought her and the next day a sable stole over a three-hundred-dollar suit of André's. She had the slimness for it, he had pointed out; she'd make a good clotheshorse. He had wanted her to spend hours, days, at the beauty places, trying out new ways of doing her hair, getting herself up to look like a fashion model. She wasn't willing to show off his success, to let the world see that Steven Graham had so much money that his wife could glitter with it.

In the cupboard there was a blue hostess gown of lovely material, a thin, faintly printed silk that hung in soft rich fullness. She dropped it over her head, and the long bishop sleeves and square neck gave her an illusion of plumpness. She had lost twenty pounds or so in these four months, but the gown had a wide wrap-around belt that could be pulled in. She stood at the mirror adjusting it, looking at herself thoughtfully. It was very queer, to be in this room and to know that Steven would never walk into it again. Never. He would never come to stand behind her at the mirror, to look over her shoulder into the glass with those slanting light-colored eyes, mocking and always guarded. Never.

She turned, went to the door, tested it to make sure it was locked. She came back to the bedroom and began to do the things she had to do, the things she had thought out carefully while she had been in prison.

There was, first, the matter of the small Yale key. It was very fortunate that on that night of Steven's death her eyes had alighted on it, lying open, unguarded, on the top of his chest of drawers beside his usual pocket collection. It had never been kept on his key ring, which was puzzling, had always been puzzling. It was the thing that had first brought it to her attention, two months at least before Steven's death. She had seen it three times; once before, she had seen it lying beside Steven's other things on the dresser, when he was bathing in preparation for an evening when they were going to the theatre and then to some party. Her mind had remarked it but without much interest, except that it was not like the tidy and careful Steven to carry a loose key. It had been shiny then, and new; and if she had thought anything she had thought that it opened a box, or a mail drawer somewhere and had been just acquired. Two weeks or so later she had seen it again, returned from the cleaners. Steven had flown to Edmonton on business, and she had sent some things to be cleaned. It had, the cleaners explained, been in a narrow inside pocket in his jacket, a specially designed pocket not usual in men's clothes; so she had missed it. She had put it back into the pocket and said nothing. But it had stayed in her mind along with a number of other things; and when, on that night of Steven's death, she had come into the bedroom and seen it—while the police were in the living room—she had dropped it casually into her jewel case when she took off the necklace and earrings she had been wearing. An old key... "I don't even remember what it opens," she had been prepared to say. If anyone asked. No one had.

She opened the white kidskin jewel case and the key

was there lying openly on the blue velvet of the bottom, along with some oddments of unimportant things. The good jewelry Steven had bought for her was fitted carefully into its proper niches; the sapphire earrings, the big emerald clips and the bracelet to match—maybe not quite the real thing, but astonishingly important-looking—the pearls and the clip watch set with diamonds. But the key lay with the enamel fleur-de-lis brooch her father had given her when she had got into high school, and the garnet pendant that had been her grandmother's, and two strings of beads, broken and awaiting attention. She lifted it out and laid it on the top of her dressing table.

Her own small desk in the corner had been thoroughly ransacked, she knew well. The police had tried to miss nothing of her life. Fortunately, one particular item, a small sheaf of canceled checks, had come to their attention on that night of the murder, and apparently never again. The checks were there, in the drawer at the left, slips of bright orange paper printed in black and all signed neatly with her name—her maiden name. H. Brown, in writing so like her own that it had been only the color of the checks that made her know they were not hers. She had never had an account in the Imperial Bank. The checks were made out for unremarkable amounts, the largest one, for three hundred dollars, being to the order of the Cortes Realty Company, which owned this penthouse apartment. Another, for ninety dollars, was to Simpson-Sears store; and in the corner, in the same neat script, was written "thirty yards orlon curtaining." A third check had gone to Lindsay's and was noted "lamps." If they had only known, that trick of identifying payments was Steven's, not hers.

They had been going through Steven's desk, on that fateful night, looking for the location of his safety-deposit box, the address of his lawyer, any possibly important letters. The officer who had come upon the checks had stood looking at them for some time. Helen, sitting dumb and dazed in her chair, had observed his intent scrutiny of them, one after the other, without any particular interest, since the sight of the orange slips at that moment had meant nothing to her. He had fixed his eyes on her living room curtains, and said with what had seemed odd inconsequence, "What're those curtains made of?" and when she had answered automatically, "Orlon," he had finished leafing through the checks and then brought them over to hand them to her. He had said, "Why would your husband be signing checks 'H. Brown,' or is that his secretary? Or what?" And Helen, answered honestly enough, "I was Helen Brown," and had followed with the instinctive guarding lie, "I have always had an account in that name." Housekeeping expenses; a woman with a separate account in her old name—perhaps it didn't seem anything remarkable. Maybe other people did the same sort of thing. Perhaps if the checks had been paid out for jewels or luxury items they would have occasioned suspicion; but rent and curtains and lamps—they were the most innocent items of living.

The checks were not innocent. Helen's name, but not her handwriting. Domestic expenses, but not hers, not for this apartment.

She stood now looking at the checks, and her heart did not ache. It held no sorrow. It was a quiet heart, dead and still, with no feeling. But her mind was not dead, and it said to her now, over and over, as it had said in prison, "There is Jamie, and there is honor." Things were bad enough. She had been tried for murder, and acquitted; the motive had fallen to pieces. But if the police had read correctly the meaning of these checks, if they had seen the key, the motive would have been infinitely stronger for her, Helen. If that field had been opened, perhaps the truth, the real truth, would have been uncovered; perhaps not. Perhaps it was too securely hidden. In any case, except as a last resort, she had known that she must be silent.

She laid the checks beside the key and went out to the kitchen. She opened the door of the cupboard over the counter which held her cookbooks and her salad bowl. She had always been a good cook, although the simple tastes of her own family ran to rare roast beef, potatoes whipped with cream and plenty of pepper, and deep apple pie. Steven had given her much instruction in the matter of food and she had learned to do all sorts of things to please him. On this deep shelf she kept turtle soup and truffles, wild rice and good spaghetti, anchovies and tiny white onions, tarragon and thyme, curry powder, hot chili. Steven liked to bring home some particular new acquaintance and impress him with the remarkable gourmet food upon which he and Helen lived. He would come in with a cold roast chicken and two or three bottles of wine and suggest that they might have Helen's special wild rice and perhaps zabaglione. Usually he did not care particularly what he ate, but the idea of gourmet eating impressed him and items of gourmet food ran trippingly from his tongue. He had been a very insecure person, Helen thought to herself, standing with the cupboard door open and surveying her supplies.

She had opened that door on the night of Steven's death, looking into the cupboard to see whether he had been home for some time, whether he had come home earlier, perhaps, and had something to eat there. But nothing had been touched. Nothing was missing. Still, her mind had told her over and over, something about that cupboard had not been just right. She had not identified the wrongness on that occasion, but it had stayed in her mind.

Now, as she looked, she saw at once what was different.

Between the Branston pickle and the consommé stood a bottle, strange and unfamiliar. It was ornate, a thing of dark red glass with a squat base and a long neck, such a bottle as she had never seen before. She reached up and took it down carefully, holding it by the top. It would hold about eight ounces, and she could not imagine of what. But it had a label, a very intricately lettered and designed label, mostly gold and black, with a small red bull and a toreador with a red cape set upon the gold. One word was lettered above the toreador, and although the letters were unfamiliar somehow, they spelled out TEQUILA.

The bottle was empty.

It had not been there on the day of Steven's death. It had not been there when she left the apartment at four in the afternoon to go to her mother's house.

It fitted into the picture forming in her mind.

The police might not have arrested her for Steven's murder on the evidence they themselves had found in the apartment. The checks had meant nothing to them; they knew nothing about the mysterious key—which, indeed, might be a quite innocent small key after all—and she had no more apparent motive to kill her husband than has any happy woman. The detective sergeant, however, had been considerably troubled about the absence of any glass close at Steven's hand. Suicides and accidental deaths didn't remove the telltale glass. The doctor had been at hand, Helen's own family doctor, old Dr. Innis; an honest, patient, kindly man who had attended her family ever since she could remember. It was he she had summoned when she had come in to find Steven so unbelievably dead, lying peacefully relaxed in what was at first glance his usual sound sleep. Since there had been nothing in her heart but pain and shock at the thought of Steven, she had telephoned his people, Matthew and his mother. The doctor had arrived first and, when he had examined Steven and asked her a few questions, had come at once to the solution of an accidental overdose of the drug that everyone knew Steven took.

"Bad stuff," Dr. Innis had said soberly. "He shouldn't have been taking it so freely, my dear. None of those drugs can be trusted; a man's judgement becomes clouded with one dose, sometimes, and he repeats without realizing that he *is* repeating. I've seen it happen time and time again."

But Steven's mother, arriving in a state of white trembling shock, would not accept his diagnosis for a second. "It was *not* an accidental overdose," she had told him flatly. "My son was exceedingly careful. He knew exactly what he was doing. That is the reason his doctor allowed him to have the drug in liquid form. Steven never made an error. He took exactly the amount his nerves demanded, not a drop more. It was *not* an accidental overdose!"

"Well, then," Dr. Innis had said gently, "I am afraid we shall have to conclude that he wished to take too much. Of the two choices, I should prefer accident."

"Do you mean...suicide?"

"I shouldn't have thought it possible. He had everything to live for."

It was at that point that her malevolence toward Helen had begun to evidence itself. "I will not accept even the mention of suicide," she said. "Steven would never have suicided. I demand that you send for the police!"

Matthew had tried to stop her. "Mother, Mother," he had said, placatingly, "Steven is dead. There's no use talking like this. Why bring in the police? Why not accept it that it's an accident?"

She had said wildly, "You fool!" and then, "If you, sir, will not telephone for the police, *I will.*"

What had motivated her, of course, Helen thought with very little feeling, was the letter that Steven had written her. She had not mentioned it at the beginning. The police had come, and she had broken a little at the sight of the blue uniforms, and Matthew had insisted on taking her home; so that during the examination of Steven's body by the police doctor, the routine examination of the apartment, Helen's rigid questioning, she had not been present. And they knew nothing of the letter. It had seemed to Helen that even the medical examiner leaned to the idea of an accidental overdose.

Then, somewhere, the question of Steven's money came into the picture; and someone had asked Helen who inherited. Remembering that will made soon after their marriage, the will she had in her jewel case, the will made almost in fun, since Steven at that moment had nothing whatever to leave, she had said innocently that she did. She was his sole heir.

It was that which began to turn the tide against her. Mrs. Graham's letter had swung it all the way up the shore until it washed over Helen completely.

The letter had been written by Steven from Edmonton, on that trip only a week before his death.

> *Mother dearest:*
> *I don't think you understand about the money. I can't do as you ask about any large amount. Maybe someday I'll be able to use it as I please, but right now I am really trapped. I'm not going to stand this too long. I'll break free. It's Helen, as you may have guessed. She is showing even more stiff-necked bitterness and determination about this money than I have seen in her before, and God knows that's saying a good deal. She has her own ideas about it and she will stop at nothing to put them into effect. As you know, out of necessity I put certain holdings in her name, and they prove to be key holdings; without*

her consent and her signature I frequently find myself in grave difficulty. If she persists in her present course I may have to take legal steps to get rid of her because I cannot tolerate her pressure. Just relax—things are coming to a head, and then when I get squared away I'll make readjustments.

As ever,

Steven

It had been damning, that letter. But Helen had sent for Mr. Pentford at once. She had not believed in Steven's money.

He had gone away, that autumn five years ago, with nothing; he had some mysterious tip about quick magnificent oil money in Edmonton. He had had to borrow the money for his plane fare. He had come home with his pockets lined with gold and more to follow. He had been extremely proud, but very guarded, and it was at that time that he had put three pieces of property in her name. Not understanding his ventures, not believing in them, she had paid little attention. She had expected it all to come to nothing. But the three leases or deeds he had signed over to her brought in amazing returns; so that he was constantly bringing her large checks for her endorsement, getting her to initial or sign all sorts of odd documents. For a long time she had gone along with him. But Steven was basically dishonest; and her conscience began to trouble her more and more. This whole matter was something she wanted to understand. Even if the holdings had not been in her name, she still wanted to know what Steven was up to. He was Jamie's father, and the thought of the penitentiary doors looming for him was not happy.

It had never occurred to her to fear them for herself. Through the letter, she could see one way in which he had used her; she was protection against his people. His mother was greedy, demanding, and the letter had been an answer to her greed. But it had also sent Helen to prison and to the courtroom to be tried for Steven's murder.

SIX

The girl at the other end of the telephone said crisply, "Cortes Realty Company."

Helen said, "I wonder if you could help me? I'm just in from out of town—Winnipeg—and some friends I can't find, rent an apartment from you.

"We have many apartments, madam. Are your friends not in the telephone book?"

"Well," Helen said apologetically, "the name is Brown. There are pages and pages of Browns in the book and a great many H. Browns."

The girl said, "Moment, please," and after a time a male voice said, "Thompson speaking."

"Mr. Thompson," Helen said, and looked steadily at herself in the wall-size mirror in the living room. "Mr. Thompson, I'm looking for some people whose name is Brown and who rent an apartment from you."

"Brown," he said gruffly. "We've got quite a few Browns, I think."

Helen put a hand to her forehead.

"How much rent do they pay?"

"Why…I don't know. I remember Mr. Brown saying that he'd sent you people a check for three hundred dollars…that was last November. I don't know whether that was one month, or a deposit, or what."

"Scarcely *one* month," Mr. Thompson replied. A little respect crept into his voice. This woman on the phone, he was obviously thinking, she must be someone…three hundred dollars a month rent, even in these days, if you could contemplate so much you must be *somebody*. "Brown," he repeated. "Seems to me…we're not supposed to give out information, you know."

"But this isn't exactly information. It's just that Brown is such a common name."

"Well," he said, grudgingly again. "Hold it a minute." He went away. Helen stared at herself in the mirror, the tall girl in the blue gown. It made her eyes look honest, that gown.

He came back. "I had an idea I remembered that check. It was a deposit. One of our bachelor flats."

"Yes," Helen said evenly.

"We have seven or eight buildings," he said. "This is one of the older ones. But convenient. Right downtown. Very convenient for coming and going."

"Yes."

"Ah," he said. "There it is. I've got it. H. Brown. They're in the building at 10 Calloran. Apartment 6, at 10 Calloran. Rented it last November first. That your friends?"

"I'm sure it is. Unless…do you have any other H. Browns?"

"No, that's the only one. We've got a Peter Blair-Brown, hyphenated, you know, and a Mrs. Kendall Brown. Other buildings. But this is the only H. Brown. I see he gave—well, now that's—he gave Steven Graham for a reference. Steven Graham…say, do you—"

"Thank you so much," Helen said gently, and placed the receiver. She sat regarding the address she had written in her neat plain writing on the pad before her. So far, so good.

She went out to the kitchen, made herself a cup of coffee, and drank it.

She rinsed her cup and put it away, thinking of Steven and his love of outward order. She was beginning to see that such order was of deep necessity to him because of his dark inward confusion. Strict meticulous order, the emphasis on elegance, on form, that had been necessary to reassure himself. He was not clean inside, not ordered, not intrinsically worthwhile...or so he deeply, secretly, had believed.

She went back to her bedroom and put on a black suit. A tall girl in a black suit, no conspicuous person. She set out on her distasteful errand.

The building at 10 Calloran, down in the center of the city, had probably been one of the first smart apartments in town. Its original red brick had been painted white for many years. She found the right entrance.

She stopped at the bottom step and drew a long breath. Upstairs there would be Apartment 6...and inside it...what? A woman, waiting? Surely not. No woman could avoid knowing that Steven was dead. Not waiting, after four months. What, then, would she be doing? Helen took the small key from her purse and fingered it. It might not open the door upstairs after all.

As she stood there, the door to the caretaker's apartment opened and a woman, tired, middle-aged, heavyset, emerged. She wore a gray overall apron and had in her hand a floor polisher. She glanced at Helen and said pleasantly enough, "Was you looking for somebody?"

"Do you have people named Brown in this part of the building?"

The woman's face went blank. "People named Brown rents number 6. But they aren't here. They never was here much. You a friend of theirs?"

Helen caught the undertone. She said, "Well, no, as a matter of fact. I'm just trying to catch up with them on a business matter."

"Bill collector?"

"No, no exactly. Is...has neither of them been around lately?"

"Haven't been around, and I don't think they're

going to be around. I think they cleared out. Say—if it's business, who were they, anyway? I never saw the likes of it. They must've had lots of money."

"Oh?"

"Didn't care what they threw away. Didn't care what they spent on the place. And just about never came near it. You know what? I never laid eyes on him at all. And I only saw her once, to really see her."

"Do you have a key to the apartment?"

The woman flushed. "No, I haven't. That's funny too. People always leaves a key with the caretaker, in case of fire, or deliveries, or pipes breaking. It's a rule of the house. But *they* didn't leave a key. And it's a funny new kind of lock. They changed it. I can't help bein' curious, and responsible and all. I tried all my keys. But they don't fit."

"I want very much to get in."

The woman had nice eyes. They were bothered now, but her intentions were good. "I can't help you. I can't get in myself." Then, "What is the trouble?"

Helen said nothing. After a moment the woman nodded, answering some question inside herself. "I kind of thought it was that." Then, "Men acts like that, you know. I been caretaking around apartments a long time. I ain't got much use for men. I don't know what drives them." She shifted the polisher to her other hand. "I wish I could help you. But I haven't got no key."

"I have a key I want to try."

The woman said slowly, "You better go along and try it. I'll just polish the hall down here."

"Thank you."

"There's some things…" She called after Helen up the stairs. "My name's Cartright, you want any help."

Number 6 was at the end of the hall. The door was painted white. Helen took out the key and fingered it again. She put it into the small shiny lock, and it fitted.

She turned it and opened the door.

The apartment was not large, and it was dusty. Doors hung open. The living room was of a good size, and the orlon curtains, full and soft, hung all across one end, covering windows and the strips of wall between them. They were rather pretty curtains, of a delicate shade of pink, and the walls were painted the same color. There were two exquisite turquoise lamps. (A hundred dollars apiece, Helen reminded herself.) Through an open door to the right she caught sight of the bedroom. It held a Continental bed, neatly made and heaped with satin cushions, pink and white and turquoise. On the dressing table was a half-empty bottle of iridescent nail polish and a crumpled paper tissue. The drawers were empty. The man's chest held nothing.

There was nothing in the highboy in the living room, nothing on the floor or on the small desk.

Can you reconstruct a woman from delicate pink curtains, a satin bed, a bottle of nail polish? What else was in this place to tell her or the woman? The woman who might be the key to everything, to her own past, to Jamie's future?

It was very soon after Steven had come back from his year in the West, his blindingly successful year, that she had begun to sense the presence of other women in his life. Until then he had been unfailingly sweet to her. It had been labor, in the Graham house, trying to make ends meet, trying to keep up the semblance of gentility and of social importance that was the breath of life to all the Grahams. Steven had needed her, and he had apparently appreciated her. Maybe, Helen thought with the first trace of bitterness she had felt for a long time, maybe that had just been his way of getting her to work. Whatever it was, she had been convinced of his appreciation, his love, his urgency toward her. But when he came back from the West and the money came pouring in from those miraculous ventures which had all succeeded, he had begun to change. At times he was almost insolent. He did not need her. Understanding the Grahams a little, she had thought it was only the insolence of success. Now the pattern was clearer. There had been other women; women who did not know the painful sordid details of his poverty, of his failure; women to whom he could be big and important, the great, the glamorous, the wonder-boy Steven Graham. And his urgency toward her had gone; his caresses had been perfunctory. What that means, Helen told herself, is that, while his arms are about you and his lips are on yours, his mind, almost his body, is with someone else. As time goes by you withdraw of necessity. You realize that it is not you he is loving; you are nothing but the shape of a woman whom he can invest with different characters at will. You are not yourself.

It had been very painful. But with the beginning of realization began also the beginning of the establishment of herself apart from Steven. To save herself she had to shut herself away from him, become invulnerable. That he hated. To feel that he could no longer attract her, no longer compel her, was a thing to make him furious. And perhaps he had some small conscience left; so that his sense of guilt made him hate her.

Would he have killed himself, because he hated her? No.

This woman was scarcely the first of his attempts to prove Steven Graham a big man.

She may not have been the last.

A jealous woman is a dangerous thing.

Who was she? She must have another life, too. There was no real living in this apartment, there had been none. There were no dishes…only a silver pitcher there on the table, some glasses.

Helen went out to the hall, to the top of the stairs. "Mrs. Cartright?"

The woman below straightened. She glanced up, set her polisher against the wall, and tiptoed up. "Not that anybody'd hear me," she said. "Everybody here's out all day. What can I do?"

Helen led the way back to the empty apartment. She shut the door.

Mrs. Cartright was staring. "Well, my soul," she said, "Pink silk and white satin—it don't look much like being lived in and having cabbage and pork chops for supper, does it? I guess that wasn't what—I guess it's what you call one of them—" She stopped.

"You said you saw her once."

"I shouldn't rightly ought to talk. But it looks like they're gone for good. Aren't they?"

"Yes. For good."

"You—you planning to—to get...to do something about it?"

"I'm just trying to tidy things up. There's nobody else to do it. These things"—she indicated the room— "they belong to her, I suppose. If I knew who she was, perhaps I might send them to her."

Mrs. Cartright stared at her. "She'd get a shock."

"It wouldn't be a kind thing to do."

"You think of kindness?"

"So much depends on who she is. I don't know. What did she look like?"

"I don't know as I can tell you exactly. Kind of pretty. Light-colored hair. Fluttery, maybe. But the day she was here...she was so scared. Anybody could see that. Scared and in a hurry."

"What did she come for?"

"She was tidying things up too. She gathered up a lot of stuff and cleared out the place." Her eyes dropped.

"Did she take things away with her?"

"No. She—well, no."

Helen put her hand out and touched the other

woman's shoulder. "Perhaps she gave them to you?"

Mrs. Cartright flushed painfully. "It's like this. I never had very pretty things, and sometimes when people move away—I mean to say—people is all different. Sometimes people think things isn't worth anything, and throw them away. But to other folks, them things is worth a lot. So I always figger—if people throw things away, they're through with them. And if I can use them, it don't hurt to take them. Only, this time…"

"How was it different?"

The woman took a long breath. "You wait here," she said, and went downstairs. In a short time she was back, and in her hands was a large dress box. "She left this, tied up just this way," she explained. "It's from Poirier's. They don't sell anything cheap. I just thought—maybe there was a few things I could use. She put it in the garbage cupboard."

"May I see?"

Mrs. Cartright untied the string carefully, as if she had tied and untied it a good many times before. "I never saw anything so pretty," she said. She lifted the lid off the box. "Maybe this was what made me feel there was really something awful wrong."

Inside the box, under the tissue paper, was a filmy garment of cherry red. Mrs. Cartright took it out with careful fingers. It was a negligee, exquisitely cut, handmade, a costly and beautiful garment. Its underslip was lace.

Mrs. Cartright held it up against her. "It don't go with my color or shape," she said. "It's about six sizes too small. But—it seemed awful pretty. I didn't have the heart to throw it away."

"I don't blame you," Helen said soberly. "What size is it?"

"Well, I take an eighteen, especially around the middle. I think this must be a ten or a twelve. I—I was thinking, maybe I could slit the slip up the back and sew a piece of something in, and the dress is open at the front anyways, over the lace. Then I could see how silly...where would I ever wear it? But I never saw anything prettier. I couldn't throw it away. Maybe, I thought, if I went on one of them diets—but where would I wear it anyway, me?"

"I don't think it's ever been worn."

"Me neither. See, the hem's just pinned up."

Helen took the negligee and carried it to the window. The hem was pinned up expertly but not sewn. So. The woman had bought it and had the fitter pin it. "I can put a hem in," she had probably said. She would have had to avoid delivery, either immediate or deferred, after the hem had been put in. So she could sew a little, this woman of the pink curtains and the cherry gown. She had tastes that were a little flamboyant...she could sew...

"She's about five foot four, I think," Helen decided. She stood with the gown in her hands, thinking. She glanced at the box. She said abruptly, "Was there a bill?"

"Well—I don't know," Mrs. Cartright said doubtfully.

She lifted out the crumpled tissue paper and shook it. Fragments of paper scattered to the rug. Some of them looked like note paper. Seeing them, Helen's heart gave a bound.

Mrs. Cartright bent and picked up a crumpled wad. She straightened it out. "Oh, my lands," she said. "No wonder it's pretty!"

Helen took the bill. The cherry gown had cost a hundred and eighty-five dollars. It had been bought on the fifth of January, two days before Steven's death. Bought...brought here, but there hadn't been time to put the hem in, or lack of foresight had not brought along the thread...maybe Steven had never seen the gown.

"A hundred and eighty-five dollars!"

There was no name on the bill. Helen put it into

her purse. She got down and sat on the floor beside the torn bits of paper there. There were nine pieces and they fitted together easily.

> *My Sweet: I leave you the money for the cherry gown. I hope it's as pretty as you say it is. I'll be along Friday night about nine. Until then, darling...*
>
> S.

On Friday night...about nine...Steven had died. Not here. In his own home, resting before he dressed to come to this place, to inspect the cherry gown.

Helen got up. "Mrs. Cartright, I'm going to pay you for this gown. You've done me a great service."

"But you can't do that! A hundred and eighty-five dollars—and it isn't rightly mine..."

"It wasn't rightly anybody's," Helen said briefly. She opened her purse. She had brought money, enough for any sort of emergency. "I'm going to send for the moving men and have all the things in the apartment packed up. But you needn't worry. Here." She rummaged in the purse again and took out the cancelled check once paid to the Cortes Realty. "You see, I am H. Brown," she said. "And if you have never seen the man...perhaps there wasn't a man. Perhaps it was just two women who came here, and I'm the one who has the right."

Mrs. Cartright's tired eyes searched her face. She said, "I don't care much anyway. If you want to do it that way. Maybe you'll send a notice to the Realty Company. I don't know what to do about this kind of thing. I'll tell them I saw the rent check. You see...my man walked out on me, too, a long time ago. If you want to do it this way. What are you going to do, send the stuff to her?"

"I don't know." Helen glanced around the room.

"You looked through everything?"

"Yes, I think so."

"People mostly forget bathrooms," Mrs. Cartright said, and started toward the inner hall. She went into the bathroom and in a moment or two came out. In her hand was a copy of a magazine and two medicine bottles. "There's some aspirin in this one," she said. "The other's empty."

Helen's eyes were fixed upon it, upon the familiar shape. She took it carefully from the woman's hand. It was an empty eight-ounce medicine bottle with a blue and white label. The label said CENTRAL DRUGS LTD. and the number was 22446. The directions: *S. Graham. One teaspoon in water at bedtime.* DO NOT REPEAT.

SEVEN

Helen turned in at the walk of her own apartment building and started toward the steps. A woman and two teen-age girls had just come out of the front door and turned toward her. Helen lifted her head. The woman—it was Mrs. Bennett, who with her family occupied the large apartment opening on the terrace at the back—Mrs. Bennett gave her a quick, startled look of recognition, then put out her hands and caught each daughter firmly by the elbow, to march them quickly past, wordless and red-faced. As they reached the sidewalk the girls bent toward their mother, obviously whispering excited questions.

Helen unlocked the wide glass door, embroidered over with its metaled filigree. The air lock took it and swung it slowly shut behind her. At the mailboxes she stopped and unlocked her own. There was one letter in it, from the Cortes Realty Company. Her mind was still on the apartment she had just left, and she stared at the letter blankly. This building, of course, was also Cortes property. She opened the letter and read it as she went up in the elevator.

> *Dear Mrs. Graham:*
>
> *We are very sorry to find it necessary to send you this notice of the termination of your lease. As you know, we reserve the right to keep our apartments filled with tenants who are satisfactory to other lessees; and we have had a number of strong complaints about your further occupancy of the penthouse. We hope that you will find other comfortable living quarters as soon as possible.*
>
> *Yours very truly,*
>
> *J. V. Mitching*

Helen read the letter over again, but it gave her no feeling save one of deepened fatigue. This sort of thing she had foreseen. All this, and much, much more. It did not matter.

She opened her own door. There were people in her living room. She stood in the doorway, surveying them. Mrs. Graham was there, stiff and upright in an armchair. Jerry stood glowering at the window. Matthew was getting up from the sofa with some difficulty.

"I was not aware that any of you had a key to my apartment."

Jerry said angrily, "They haven't got a key, any more than I have. The superintendent let them in. Then when I knocked they answered, so I got in too. Foot-in-the-door technique…they didn't want me.

Helen walked further into the room. She stood looking at her guests.

The color rushed up into the older woman's face. She said bitterly, "It has been very obvious that you do not intend to come to me."

"For what reason should I have come?"

Steven's mother looked at her icily. "I may as well make it quite clear that I have not come here to beg."

"No."

"Don't misunderstand me. I am here to demand my rights."

"I see."

"It is clear that you have been avoiding us. You refused my dinner invitation. You have not called at the house. You have not answered your telephone."

"There were some things I had to take care of."

Mrs. Graham sat a little straighter. "What is more to the point, your lawyer refuses, absolutely refuses, to discuss the matter of Steven's will with my lawyer. Refuses. The matter, he says, is closed."

"Well?"

"Don't be insolent!"

Jerry, at the window, began a tuneless low whistling. He was trying to keep his temper.

Helen said in a low voice, "I have no wish to be insolent. What is it you want, exactly, from me?"

"You know quite well what I want. My rights. That's all. My rights."

"You mean…Steven's money? Is that what you mean, exactly?"

"I most certainly do. I most certainly do."

"In his will, Steven left everything to me. You know that. A will seems to be a will, and the money is all mine…by right. Do you want to talk about rights, then, or about money?"

"You know that he made that will when he had nothing! When you were first married, when it was only a gesture! If he had made a will later, last winter for instance, you would have had your proper share and no more. You know that."

"Yes, as a matter of fact, I do," Helen admitted. "I'm quite sure of it. But he didn't make a will last winter.

This is the only will there is. He gave it to me a month after we were married as a kind of joke. You are quite right. And I kept it—fortunately. Otherwise, there would have been no will at all, and then I suppose the estate would have been divided in certain other ways."

"Trust you to keep anything you could get your hands on!"

"Mrs. Graham," Helen said steadily, "I wish you would try to be calm. I can assure you that you will gain nothing by taking this stand. It used to be that I was afraid of you…that I did what you ordered me to do because I was insecure. But that won't happen again. I have been through something of a maturing experience. To be accused of murder, to live in prison for some months, to be tried for your life, to live through long days and nights with the thought of the hangman's rope always in front of you, waiting for you when you know you are innocent…that is a maturing experience. I'm sure you can understand. You cannot frighten me, never again. Never."

The older woman leaned back in her chair.

Helen said, "If we could have met this matter of Steven's death as a family—if you had faced the situation with me instead of against me—the death of someone we all had loved…it might have been very different. I must say that I don't understand why you acted as you did, because you know quite well I am incapable of murder."

Mrs. Graham's mouth worked. She whispered, "I didn't…I wasn't…"

"You did, and you were. You knew what Steven's letter really meant, Mrs. Graham. You didn't want to know, but you knew. You were angry because you couldn't force Steven to give you more money…angry at Steven. Oh, I understand. It wasn't that you deliberately planned to have me arrested—you didn't think anything out. You were just wildly angry, angry at everybody. And when you're angry you accuse everyone of everything. I know. But you see," she said soberly, "you shouldn't have done it."

Matthew, sitting limp in his chair, had a strange smile on his face as he stared at his mother.

"If you hadn't had me arrested," Helen said steadily, "I shouldn't now be in the position I am in. I have been acquitted, but I'm still guilty in many minds. And I'm Jamie's mother. I don't know exactly what's going to happen, but I'm going to keep every penny of Steven's money—if it turns out to be really his money—to make a decent life for Jamie if I need to."

There was a long dead silence. Then at last Matthew said, "What do you mean, if it turns out to be Steven's money?"

"You know what I mean," Helen said wearily. "You know I'm having all his affairs investigated. I started that last autumn. But we couldn't get very far while Steven held most of the papers. Now we are making progress. There may not be any money, you know, Mrs. Graham. You know Steven better than I do. Maybe he doesn't own a penny of all he apparently had."

"I don't know what you mean. I don't understand you at all."

"Oh yes, you do," Helen said.

Matthew said heavily, "She understands, all right. We all know what little Stevie was. Never knew him to tell the truth when a lie would do. Never knew him to keep his hands off other people's property if he could get them on it. Never knew him to play square on anything. That was our Stevie. If he could've turned a crooked deal, he would've done it. So you're likely smart to have it all looked into—before somebody else does and catches up on Steve. Smart. Mother, come on home. You're wasting your time. I told you so. You're just wasting your time."

EIGHT

Police Constable Henry Lake walked crisply up the garden path of Dr. Jonathan Merrill's home, toward the door in the east wing which, as he knew from long experience, opened into the office. His eyes noted the greening of the grass and the purple hyacinths in hardy bloom in the bed along the front of the house, but his mind was elsewhere. He always liked coming to this place, but upon this occasion he was particularly happy. He was, actually, elated. And with reason.

He twisted the old-fashioned bell set into the front door, and without waiting for a command let himself into the small hallway. This old house on Prince Albert had been in the Merrill family for donkey's years, built by the professor's grandfather back in the days when there was nothing much north of College Street. It had been quite an estate, the Merrill place; even yet the remains of the big stables, three blocks away, were serving as a smart modern apartment set on a short street known as Merrill Lane. The professor was about forty, probably; he'd grown up here, and as a child he would have kept his pony in those stables.

P.C. Lake tapped at the inner door, and Dr. Merrill's voice said gently, "Come in."

He was sitting at the far end of his desk. It always gave P.C. Lake amusement to see that desk. If a person didn't know the professor so well, and understand just a little how his mind worked, it would have been funny, that desk. It was made of three tremendous dining tables pushed together at angles, and each one was stacked, piled, with papers, pamphlets, books, bits of manuscripts that nobody could ever make head or tail of but Dr. Merrill himself. He knew what everything was and where everything was. It had sometimes appeared that on the long table toward the east he kept his university stuff, his psychology material, papers, notebooks. On the table to the west, nearest the door into his house, were his police matters. And the table at whose end he sat held the telephone, an ash tray as big as a dinner plate, and a mass of miscellaneous papers that he was always pushing around absently, coming up with what he wanted but always in a harassed way, as if he hadn't got around to sorting that tableful yet, although he'd been doing the same thing for years.

He was listening to the telephone. He looked over the cradle to P.C. Lake, nodded his head, indicated a chair, and made a muttering noise into the telephone, a sort of apologetic noise so that whoever was talking to him would catch on that he needed to get away. People told him everything on that telephone. There was something about his quietness and his believing that made everyone tell him everything.

P.C. Lake got out his notebook while he waited. He scanned his report and turned some of the information over again in his mind.

Dr. Merrill set the phone down. He ran a quick hand over his thick hair and gave P.C. Lake that quick grin, almost a conspirator's grin. You never quite knew what confidence he was letting you into, but it was confidence. He trusted everybody in a funny kind of way, probably even crooks; as if he thought of everybody as people.

He said, "Cigarette, Henry?"

"No, thank you, sir," Henry Lake said. "Not at the moment." He glanced at the notebook. "I think you will be pleased to know, sir, that you were quite right. Mrs. Graham did possess private information upon which she acted immediately on her release. I must say that at the moment it does not come just clear as to where she is going, but she is going somewhere."

"An improvement," Dr. Merrill murmured.

"Following your suggestion, sir, I took it upon myself

to keep an eye on her. Upon her release, she went directly to her apartment with her brother. Then, a little later, she went to her parents' home in Parkdale and spent the night there with them. On the following morning she returned alone to her apartment, her brother being engaged with his university examinations. He seems much attached to her and it would seem that he might wish to accompany her on whatever it is she is engaged upon, except that he is in his final year at the university, sir, as you know, and the examinations are very important to him."

"Yes."

Henry Lake frowned at his book. "My report, sir. On the morning of April 23, Mrs. Helen Graham left her apartment in her Packard coupé, it having been delivered at her request and left in her garage space in the basement of the building in which she resides. She drove the Packard north, up Bathurst Street to Wilson Avenue, and drove around on the country roads for a few miles, in an aimless manner. Finally she turned south and went directly to Calloran Street, where she entered the building known as the Calloran Arms." He glanced at the professor, who nodded.

"She was inside the building for an hour and fourteen minutes. It was subsequently ascertained that she spent most of her time in Apartment 6, to which she had a key."

"The Yale key from her jewel case? Quite possibly. It was a new key and she had no new lock that we could discover."

"As I well remember," P.C. Lake said wryly.

Dr. Merrill's eyes on P.C. Lake's face were clear and steady. He said, "This is good, Henry. Go on."

"The caretaker of the Calloran Arms is one Mrs. Cartright. She was questioned at some length, and proved a difficult witness." He stopped reading and looked at Dr. Merrill. "She seemed to have taken a strong fancy to Mrs.

Graham, sir; that was the trouble. She was afraid of my uniform…it was necessary to assure her that I was on Mrs. Graham's side in any trouble."

"She knew Mrs. Graham?"

"No, sir. She'd never seen her before and didn't seem to connect her with the Grahams at all. The name never came into it. She had been led to believe that Mrs. Graham was a Mrs. Brown. Apartment 6 was in the name of H. Brown, it seems, and Mrs. Cartright got the idea that our Mrs. Graham was the real Mrs. Brown, come to track down a great injustice that had been done her."

"I see."

Henry Lake said, "Mrs. Cartright herself was deserted by her husband ten years ago." He went on with his report. "At the time of the investigation of the Calloran Arms—another man having been detailed to follow Mrs. Graham for the time being—the door of Apartment 6 was open and two men from the furniture moving firm of Tippet Richardson's were taking down curtains, packing certain items of furniture—a bed, some lamps, a sofa, etc.—preparatory to taking them to the warehouse for storage.

Later questioning at Tippet Richardson's, after satisfactory explanations had been given to the manager, brought out the fact that the items were being stored in the name of H. Brown, whom we know as Mrs. Graham. It should be established here that there is no other H. Brown appearing in the matter."

"The checks," Dr. Merrill murmured.

"Yes, sir. You will remember that upon your instigation we inquired into the bank account, discovered that it had been opened by the mail deposit of a large check of Steven Graham's made out to H. Brown, that the manager of the bank had never seen his client, and that the only checks issued on the account were those found in the small shelf in Mr. Graham's desk.

"This Calloran Arms apartment was, you say, in the name of H. Brown?"

"Yes, sir."

"What are Tippet Richardson's orders regarding the furnishings?"

"To hold them, sir, until they receive further instructions."

"They are valuable?"

"The company has insured them for a coverage of a thousand dollars. There are few items, but they are all good. There is one box of clothing," Henry Lake said, and stopped.

"Important?"

"It contains a red dress, sir. I examined it. The moving men said that the caretaker had told them to be sure and not lose that small box...it held a gown worth a hundred and eighty-five dollars."

Dr. Merrill's eyebrows went up a little.

"I never saw a dress like it," Henry Lake said stolidly. He looked again at his notes. "In regard to the apartment, sir, certain conclusions have to be reached."

"Which are?"

"That we have here what might be called a love-nest in process of being dismantled."

Dr. Merrill regarded Henry Lake thoughtfully. He leaned back a little in his leather chair.

"You would have made further inquiries?"

"Yes, sir. After gaining some measure of Mrs. Cartright's confidence, I went as deeply as possible into the identification of the personalities involved. I have not been very successful. The man, she *thinks* she never saw. The woman was small, possibly five foot four in height and small in proportion. Fair hair, not too young, sir. Mrs. Cartright did not find her a beauty, but Mrs. Cartright is definitely prejudiced."

"Any indication of the woman's identity?"

"None."

"Did you gather that Mrs. Graham knew it?"

"On the contrary, sir, that she was trying to discover it."

Dr. Merrill smoked in silence. After a moment he said, "From where did the dress come, if it was still in a box?"

"May I come to that a bit later, sir?"

"Go on."

"I should like to keep events in chronological order in case something suggests itself to you as being explanatory. My colleague who followed Mrs. Graham from the Calloran Arms knows that when she got home the other Grahams, Mrs. Graham, Sr., and Mr. Matthew Graham were in her apartment waiting for her. He questioned the superintendent later, rather firmly; the gentleman said that since Mrs. Graham had been asked to leave he had had no compunctions about admitting the Grahams to her apartment, and he was rather insolent, sir; he says he has been under police orders about that apartment for four months now and he is tired of the whole thing."

"I don't question that," Dr. Merrill said dryly. "Well, what did the Grahams want?"

"My colleague did not know, sir. I may mention that young Jerry Brown was also present at the meeting. In any case, the Grahams left very soon after Helen Graham's arrival, and in a state of mind obviously not pleasant. Mrs. Graham looked extremely angry as they drove away, and Mr. Matthew Graham, driving the car, went through two stop lights on the way home and was intercepted and warned at the corner of Bloor and Sherbourne."

"He shouldn't be allowed to drive at all, our Matthew," the professor said thoughtfully.

"No, sir. And now…" He took a deep breath. "To make a long story short, sir, may I report that in regard to the dress I myself followed up the matter. On the day following her discovery of the apartment, that is, day before yesterday, Mrs. Graham herself went to Poirier's, which is the exclusive ladies' shop from which the red gown apparently came. She herself bought a gown; but her purpose was to discover the identity of the woman who bought the red dress. She was not successful. Poirier's do not know. But we both discovered, Mrs. Graham first and myself following her, that the small fair woman with a beautiful figure—I quote the salesperson, sir—comes from Mapleton and is a member there of the country club set. She remarked to the saleswoman that the red gown would create quite a sensation at the country club ball—although it was a negligee she thought she would wear it to the dance. She is not known at Poirier's, having made but two purchases there: the red gown and, last November, a mink stole, for which she paid seven hundred dollars in large bills. It is rather unusual, I gather, for Poirier customers to pay cash; most of them have charge accounts. The woman on both occasions has been the subject of a certain curiosity. They therefore remember her."

"There are certainly conclusions to be drawn from that information, Henry."

"Yes, sir." Henry Lake looked up expectantly.

"Was the gown much worn?"

"It was new."

"Yet the woman did not take it away with her to her own home. She took the mink stole. A curious situation."

"Yes, sir."

"It would seem that she could explain one luxurious item and not another. Or that the red gown came at an inopportune time. When was it bought?"

"Sir, two days before Steven Graham's death. It had never been worn."

"I see," Dr. Merrill said. He stood up and went to

look at the window, his slight figure outlined against the long glass. The windows in this room began at the floor, in the old-fashioned manner. Either housebreakers had been uncommon in the old days, or the long shutters were always locked at dark.

Henry Lake said, "What it seems to me, sir, is that we have here a married woman engaged in an intrigue which she must of course keep from her husband. I do not understand what she did with the mink stole, unless it is in storage somewhere. My understanding is that it is difficult for a woman to keep mink in storage."

"I have heard something of the kind," Jonathan Merrill said.

"The woman's husband may not be wealthy, but he must be comfortably off for them to live in Mapleton and belong to the country club set."

"Yes."

"Mapleton is not a large town. Its population is about four thousand people, sir."

Merrill turned. He said, "Astonishing that no hint of this particular entanglement came into police hands. The woman and Graham were never seen together; I remember certain other women who were carefully investigated. This one has never been suspected."

"No, sir."

"As a matter of curiosity," Dr. Merrill said, "how was it that those checks were passed over until you and I found them just before Helen Graham's release?"

"They were not passed over, sir. She was questioned about them. But her manner was easy, her acceptance of them immediate; and the items for which they had paid were so completely domestic, even to the name of the realty company, which also rents her own apartment. They were not suspicious items, sir. And as you point out, no whisper of this important other woman had reached the ears of any of us."

Dr. Merrill came back to his chair and sat down, lit a cigarette and stared thoughtfully at Henry Lake. He said, "So there is a woman, with a reasonably successful husband. She is not young. We must gather that the husband likewise is not young. Graham was young, handsome, wealthy, a practiced Lothario. He would have been a serious menace to what may have been for years a happy marriage. The fact that secrecy was so essential, and that the attachment was so strong as to cause him to rent an apartment, furnish it expensively, and buy mink and a costly negligee suggests that it was no passing fancy. Obviously Mrs. Graham suspects its importance." The clear eyes met those of Henry Lake.

"Sir."

"Yes?"

"You do not incline to suicide. Nor do you believe that Steven Graham died accidentally."

"The amount of the drug was far too great for accident. It was deliberate, Henry. We know that. It has been possible to suggest that the size of the lethal dosage varies greatly with different individuals…it has been possible to play down that part of the picture a little, in the interests of future investigation. But we all know that somehow, somewhere, Steven Graham got a deliberately administered lethal dose—administered possibly by himself, we must still admit that, however incredible it seems. But deliberate, not accidental." He stopped. "So far there has appeared no hand, except that of his wife's, which might have administered that dose. But, more fortunately, it was not possible to prove that his wife's hand gave him the dose. I must say, Henry, that I don't blame anyone who still suspects her. If I did not know her…if I were not sure of her…" He stopped.

"Sir," Henry Lake said, and took a long breath.

"Yes?"

"I *may* have a description of the person we have to search for."

Dr. Merrill's hand was still, holding his cigarette.

"Upon once occasion, Mrs. Cartright *did* see a man at the door of Apartment 6. She had never seen this Mr. H. Brown who was supposed to be renting the apartment. She was very curious about him. But just before Christmas she thought she had seen him at last. She came into the upper hall unexpectedly," Henry Lake said.

"And?"

"This man was straightening from the door, as if he had just shut it. She said to him, 'Oh…I guess it's Mr. Brown, is it? I'm the caretaker.' And he said at once that he wasn't, sir. He said he was the census taker."

"There was no census being taken at that time."

"No, sir."

"Was the man Steven Graham?"

"No, sir. He was a much older man than Steven Graham, a short man, broad, with a flat face. Sort of a dark face, she said. Definitely not Steven Graham."

"Was she sure he had just come from the apartment?"

"No, sir. It was her impression that he had just locked the door. He said no, he had just been knocking. She hadn't heard any knocking. And he didn't attempt to visit any other apartments, to continue with the census."

Jonathan Merrill pulled a piece of paper toward him and picked up a thick yellow pencil. He began to make intricate curlicues all over the paper.

"I think you had better go yourself to Mapleton, Henry. We had better hurry a little. The girl is not afraid. She is on the track of something very important to her. I am sure it is not idle curiosity about her husband's amours which prompts her. She is very intelligent. She knows quite well what her position is in the public mind. She loves her child. She is a person who has always enjoyed a clean name and reputation; it will seem important to her to re-establish herself. I doubt if it occurs to her that in doing so she will uncover a hand that has already been driven once to extremity, in order to protect something of value to itself. In other words," he said soberly, "I doubt if she understands murder."

"No, sir," Henry Lake said, and stirred in his chair.

"It looks fairly simple, after what you've uncovered. A family man, short, broad, with a flat dark face, with a beautiful wife; a man who at some point of his career was perhaps a census taker. A man who may appear to have been fooled but who has not been fooled; who perhaps from the beginning had a duplicate of his wife's key to the secret apartment. A man, one would gather, of considerable guile. A jealous man, a man of strong and hidden emotion."

Henry Lake got up. He settled his tunic carefully. He said, "I was hoping you'd want me to go to Mapleton, sir."

"You'd better get along, then, Henry. If Mrs. Graham continues in this direct way of hers, she may well be there before you." He took a long breath. "She is a thoughtful and intelligent young woman. It is unfortunate that she met this Graham when she was young and believing. It is very unfortunate."

NINE

Helen drove up St. George Street slowly, thread-threading her way home through the heavy afternoon traffic, after a visit to her mother, a thoughtful visit and a long talk over her living situation and Jamie. Passing the red brick structure which housed the Department of Psychology, she caught sight of a tall man coming down a flight of steps; it was Jonathan Merrill.

There was a woman with him, a small pleasant figure, her face upturned to his, her arm linked in his. Probably his sister, Helen thought absently. She was a clever girl, Jonathan Merrill's sister, people said, who worked closely with him. But Helen paid her little attention. The sight of Jonathan Merrill was a coincidence, something like a pointing finger. Would it be wise to go to the police with this situation she had discovered? She had been turning it over in her mind now for twenty-four hours. Was it not in a sense her duty to go to the police? She had found with small difficulty a strong entanglement which had lain about Steven at the time of his death; she knew where he had intended going on that very evening. Might it not be that this was the end of the thread that might unravel the truth?

No, no, never the police.

Then, Jonathan Merrill?

Well, was he to be trusted? If he had any power, why had he not assuaged the vindictive anger of the Prosecuting Attorney? Why had he, having talked to her, having been called into her case, why had he allowed her to come to trial? If he were truly wise, and if he had any authority, he must have known her to be innocent. People liked Jonathan Merrill and said kind things about him; perhaps they were just fooled by his position in the Department of Psychology, by his quiet manner, by his appearance. No. He had done nothing for her. He would do nothing for her.

There was no one to trust.

At the corner of St. George and Bloor she stopped the car and sat for a long time, thinking things out. At last she got out and went into the drugstore at the Medical Arts, to find a pay telephone. She called the number of the Graham house; Matthew answered.

"Matthew? It's Helen."

"Well, good Lord," he said.

"I'd like very much to have a talk with you. Will you have dinner with me tonight at the flat?"

"Well, I—well, of course! Delighted. You mean, just me? Not Mother?"

"Just you. At seven?"

"I'll be there. What—I mean to say, has Pentford—that is—"

"At seven," Helen repeated, and hung up. She went back to the car and drove on north to Dupont Street and the liquor store. There was shopping to do if Matthew was coming to dinner.

She came away from the liquor store with a bottle of good rye, one of scotch, a pint bottle of Drambuie, and a smaller bottle of crème de menthe. At Scott's, farther along the street, she stopped for her food. She knew Matthew's tastes very well. He was not a particularly good trencherman but his appetite could be tempted. She bought filet mignon, mushrooms, and red and green peppers for her own special steak sauce. There was no point in considering dessert; he had no respect for sweets.

At the apartment, she drove the car into the garage and went up in the elevator, unobserved, inoffensive. Inside her own four walls she set the table. She found four long mahogany-colored candles to go into the pottery candlesticks. She unwrapped the steak, cooked wild rice, made her steak sauce, and put it into the wide-mouthed jug. She prepared the mushrooms. She set out all the necessary dishes and utensils. Then she unwrapped her liquor and filled the decanters in the locked tantalus Steven had owned before his marriage—two square crystal bottles set into a silver frame whose handle, crossed on itself and locked, made the contents of the bottles unavailable to anyone who did not have the key. In this place, in his own home, Steven had never locked the tantalus and the key was long ago lost. But in the Graham house the tantalus had always been locked and the key had lived on Steven's ring. Matthew hated the thing and always had. He considered it a personal insult—as, in a sense, it was. It had been bought because of him. Now, Helen thought, she would set it in front of him, unlocked, specially filled for him and for him only.

When the meal was organized it was almost half past six. Her new violet gown was lovely, lying ready on the gray satin spread. She bathed, and then went to inspect carefully the row of perfume bottles on her dressing table. She usually forgot about perfume, but Steven had loved it and bought it practically by the quart for her. There had been a time when his gifts had warmed her heart, when she had taken them as evidence of his love; but she knew now, had known for years, that they meant only that his conscience was particularly clouded at the moment and that, too, he felt insecure and found it necessary to pay a little insurance, to buy her loyalty.

She chose tonight one of the fragrances she liked best: Lanvin's Arpège. It was not Steven's favorite; his tastes ran to heavier, darker scents. But Matthew, oddly enough, in many ways had a greater delicacy of taste than Steven. Matthew, Helen thought as she soaked a small pad of cotton in the perfume and rubbed it on her throat, behind her ears, in the curve of her elbows—Matthew was a tragedy. He was intelligent. He had more brains than Steven. He had in his time and for short periods held down any number of jobs that called for quick thinking, a sensitive approach, an eye and a mind for relationships. Of late years he had not held any of them for long, but he still occasionally came out with a reference to some person, some situation, that had been part of his life and that could have had real importance had he not been the victim of his own indulgences.

She had just fastened the narrow silver buckle at the waist of the violet gown when the door buzzer sounded.

Matthew looked at her in sharp astonishment. His

eyes traveled down the violet gown and up again. "Well!" he said in ungrudging admiration. "I must say that's a honey of a dress. I never saw you look so beautiful!"

"Thank you very much," Helen said calmly. She held the door wide. He came in, still looking at her. "You confuse me," he said. "An invitation to dinner, and now a remarkable new dress—is this all for me?" He glanced round the room. "Nobody else coming, or is the stage set just for me?"

"Nobody else is coming," Helen assured him. He was sober. Probably the money situation was stringent, Helen decided. In a few days he would start selling things out of the house, but he hadn't quite come to that yet.

She saw the glance he sent across the room to the small lowboy upon which the tantalus always sat. She said easily, "Matthew, will you pour yourself a drink while I'm in the kitchen for a minute or two? I won't be long."

"Fine," he said, and went across to the tray. He looked well from the back; he was tall enough, not as tall as Steven, but almost six feet, and he had a good figure. His face sagged a good deal, with pouches under the eyes and a general look of slackness. But from the back he looked a sound man.

He called to her in a minute or two, "Shall I make you a drink, and if so, what?"

"A little rye and ginger ale," she replied. She turned the heat on in the broiler and got the steak from the refrigerator. There was no use hurrying the dinner, as she knew well. Matthew would not be content with one drink, or two, and she was quite willing to have him satisfy himself tonight. She went back to the living room and sat down in the armchair beside the window. Matthew brought her drink and then settled himself comfortably in the chair nearest the tantalus. He raised his glass. "Well, here's to whatever you have in mind," he said cheerfully. "Especially if it's cut to fit around that extremely charming gown."

Helen said, "I *have* something in mind—and I thought you might be able to help me—you know Toronto so well, Matthew, and the environs, and you know a great many people, too."

He gave her a quick careful glance. It was a look she had seen many times before Steven's death. Matthew wondered quite obviously how much she really knew of Steven's faithlessness, or if she knew anything; and, if she asked, or tried indirectly to find out anything from him, how much he should tell.

"You know that I'm leaving the apartment," she said. "I've been trying to decide where to go and what to do."

"I see," he said, and leaned back. A faint importance crept over him. She was asking his advice. After all, she could hear him thinking, after all, he was the head of the family—her husband's family, her son's family. He said, "Doesn't it depend pretty much on what they find about Steven's money?"

She did not answer for a moment. Matthew said, "I don't really blame you for feeling the way you do about that money. Mother was pretty rough on you when you and Steven lived at the house. She never treated you as if you were his wife. She can't see now that you are. It is completely impossible for my mother to see that something which was once hers, as Steven was, could ever belong to anyone else." He said carefully, "How did you think I could help you?"

"I've been asked to leave the apartment, and it's no good anyway, for Jamie. And I want him home with me. So I've been thinking of buying a house, and preferably outside the city. I thought you might tell me the best place to go."

"I see," he said.

"I don't want to live in the city. I'd like Jamie to have

a freer life than he can have in the city." She lifted her eyes. "Do you know any people in Mapleton?"

He showed no trace of shock, or of a necessity to hide anything. "Well, yes. I suppose I know quite a few people in Mapleton. It's the best of the towns close by. It's got a lot of pleasant homes and it's quite a cultural center. It has a good community sense. There's a little theater operating, and I know the country club is very popular. Chap I used to work with when I was doing advertising—Burke Patterson, the artist—lives in Mapleton. He's a friend of mine. Maybe you know his work…"

"He's an illustrator, isn't he? A good one."

Matthew nodded. "That's the lad."

"Do pour yourself a drink, Matthew. Nothing is spoiling…I'll cook the steak when you're ready. Was Burke Patterson a friend of Steven's?"

"No, they didn't know each other, except casually. Steven came home last summer and said he'd seen Burke out there and Burke asked after me. They'd met maybe once or twice here in town, that's all."

"Oh," Helen said lightly. "I don't think I remember Steven going to Mapleton."

"It was when you were in Muskoka, I think. August. He went out to play golf with somebody, I forget who." He poured the scotch carefully into his glass and came back to sit down. He was quite the man of the world, relaxed, with the unlocked tantalus within reach.

"Did he have any business connections there?"

"I don't know," Matthew said. "I don't think so." He took a long appreciate sip from his glass. "That's extremely good scotch," he said. "You're being extraordinarily sweet to me tonight, my dear. Would you like to drive out to Mapleton and look the place over? I'll go with you, if you want me to, and we'll call on Burke."

"Tomorrow?"

"Fine."

"I'll pick you up."

"Afternoon?"

"About three o'clock. If that's all right."

"That's fine," he said. "I am not seriously busy at the moment." He took a long breath. "I shall have to face the family finances at any time now. Unfortunately, it is quite impossible for me to earn enough money at any job to keep things going as Mother needs them. It always has been. Anything I could produce was only a small drop in a big bucket. I am not quite excusing myself for a certain lack of drive. I gave up trying long ago." He said unhappily, "I wish you would marry me and make a man of me, Helen. It would—oh, hell," he muttered. "I didn't mean that. You wouldn't marry me and I wouldn't like any making-over process. I've been pretty well processed all my life as it is. It's not a good thing to be forced to live in the rigid pattern that someone else wants. I didn't even know until I was grown up that I could have developed a pattern of my own. Then it was too late."

"Matthew."

"Yes?"

"Neither you nor your mother had anything to do with Steven's death, had you?"

His eyes went wide. "Good God, no," he said. "You ought to know that."

"Yes, yes—I do."

TEN

The kitchen of the Graham house in Rosedale was not particularly convenient, not even very well lighted, but Beatrice the cook took care that it was always spotless. She sat now behind the table in the breakfast nook, clean and fresh in her white uniform. She was eating with great gusto the large steak on the plate set on the yellow-flowered plastic cloth. She swallowed a mouthful, laid down her fork, and looked at Jane, finishing her coffee across the table. She said, "I never ate so much food in my life, as since you started me on this meat diet! And you know—it doesn't make sense, but I've lost two pounds!" She put a hand down to the belt of her uniform, and she could almost get her finger inside it. "I *feel* thinner," she said, "And I'm not hungry. I'm never a bit hungry."

"That's what's supposed to happen," Jane said cheerfully. "You live on meat, fat meat and all, mostly steak and rare roast beef, and you'll feel wonderful and you'll get thin. Only…you won't cheat a bit, will you, Beatrice? When you're cooking, not even a taste of the sauces or the desserts."

"I know," Beatrice said. "No salt, no sugar, no flour. But it doesn't make good sense, Jane. It's so *much* food, and it's so good. I really am getting a little thinner already, and I feel so good. I don't care how much it costs. If I could only get thin…and walk into a store and buy a size fourteen…even a sixteen…even an *eighteen*," she said generously, "I'd be the happiest girl on earth. And you know what I'd do?"

Jane filled her cup again. She was keeping an ear out for sounds in the rest of the house. It was only eight o'clock, and Mrs. Graham usually did not come down until nine. Matthew was unpredictable. But he had come in at a respectable hour last night, twenty minutes past eleven, and he had been cheerful and apparently practically sober. He had spent the evening with his sister-in-law. Mrs. Graham would certainly be a mass of intense curiosity and might take a notion to come down any minute and demand that Matthew be called too. Jane went back to the kitchen table with her coffee. She said,

"What would you do, down at a size fourteen?"

"Well, first thing…I'd go to some nice respectable place where they dance square dances, and I'd learn how. I always wanted to dance a square dance and I think I could. I'd get me a real full skirt, with big flowers all over it, and one of those peasant blouses with a lot of cross-stich embroidery. I can do cross-stich. I've got a lot of embroidery put away," Beatrice said wistfully. She picked up her coffee cup. "I don't really like coffee without cream, that's for sure," she said.

"Look in the bottom of the cup and see yourself square-dancing around with a handsome cattleman from Calgary and forget the cream."

Beatrice smiled, and the dimples in her cheeks deepened. "If it works out that you and me are together for a while, I'll get there. But you know, Jane—I'm not so dumb, and I can see with half an eye that you're not what you look like. You've got brains and looks and zip and all kinds of bright ways and notions…" She sat looking at Jane speculatively. "I've been turning it all over and over in my mind but I can't put two and two together. Sometimes I wonder…" Her voice trailed off, and her eyes on Jane were filled with thoughtful conjecture.

"Sometimes you wonder what?"

"Well…look how you came here three weeks ago. I get to wondering—after all, I can read. Things don't really happen the way the books say, but I get to wondering if—well, it may sound silly, but in the books you'd be planted here in the house to find out what you could find about Mr. Steven."

"My goodness, you do read the shockers, don't you?" Jane said. "What would I be trying to find out, for instance?"

"That's what I don't know," Beatrice said slowly. "I don't see what there could be to find out. It isn't as if either Matthew or his mother would've killed Mr.

Steven—if he was killed. His mother worshiped the ground he walked on, always did. I've been here two years, and I know. She hated his wife mostly because she was jealous, but she just worshiped Steven. He was a nasty piece of goods, too," Beatrice said flatly. "Worse than Matthew, you come right down to it, because he had a fine good-looking wife, a nice girl, and he just fooled her right and left."

"Is that for sure?" Jane said lightly.

"Of course it's for sure. Why—even last summer—" She stopped.

"Don't leave me hanging in mid-air," Jane said. "After all, I'm grown up, Beatrice. I know the facts of life."

"Well, last summer—Mrs. Graham had been up north. She got Steven to give her the money. And it was the week end when Matthew took the car and went up to get her, so there wasn't anybody here in the house but me. Mr. Steven came here with—" She stopped, flushing.

"What did he do, bring a friend here?"

"That's it," she said. "I guess he kind of forgot about me, or else he thought I was out. I was up on the third floor, in my room, and I knew all the doors was locked. I'd taken a bath and was lying down in my kimono, just having a real good rest. All of a sudden I heard voices, a man and a woman, and at first I thinks to myself, 'It's old Mrs. Graham and Matthew.' But Matthew'd only just gone that morning so it didn't make sense. Well, I listened."

"*I* certainly would have listened," Jane announced with truth. "You had to, when it comes to that. You were in charge of the house."

"Yes, of course I had to. But I would've anyway," Beatrice said honestly. "They were laughing, having a wonderful time. I got my clothes on, soon as I recognized

Mr. Steven's voice, but I didn't make a sound. I wasn't supposed to be on duty, so I just kept still."

"What did they do?" Jane inquired easily.

"Well…I wasn't down there. They—they stayed on the ground floor for quite a while," Beatrice explained. "I could hear Steven getting ice cubes out of the refrigerator. They had drinks, I guess, but there wasn't any glasses for me to wash. That Steven—I must say, he's about as neat a man as you'd ever want to meet. Was, I mean. He never threw his clothes around. Of course, he didn't live here much after I came, but a few times he was here for a few days, some reason or another, his wife visiting her family, or something. And his room was a bandbox. He kept his cupboards like a woman."

"Like *some* women," Jane said ruefully.

"Well, like some women. And he'd come to the kitchen to get a drink and if the water splashed in the sink he'd find the cloth and wipe up every drop, even there in the sink. And he always washed and dried the glass and put it away. I don't know what there was about him, but he was just neat beyond words. So that day he'd washed the glasses, like always, and put the ginger-ale bottle in the garbage. Gin and ginger ale they had, and at first I thought they'd taken their drinks upstairs with them—" she stopped. She pressed her lips together.

"So they went upstairs," Jane said. "When was this, Bee?"

Beatrice considered. "I guess maybe about the middle of August."

"You didn't get a look at the woman at all?"

"Not close up. But…well, I couldn't help being curious. I guess at first I hoped it was his wife. It didn't sound like her, though, not from the first. The voice was sort or little and fluttery. It wasn't Helen."

"I couldn't have stood not seeing her. I'd have watched out the front window when they were leaving."

"Well, that's what I did," Beatrice said. "I waited till I heard water running, a while later, and heard them talking. Then I slipped into the front bedroom—your room—and watched. And after a while they came out and went down the walk. He looked real handsome, like he always did, tall and with that swinging walk, and the broad shoulders. And she—"

"Was she small, like her voice?"

"Well, of course I was looking down on them. I couldn't really tell how tall she was. I think about up to his shoulder. Not as tall as his wife. But what you really couldn't miss was her figure. She looked like a model. She walked like one too. And she had on a white dress, no sleeves, and a big lacy black hat and black gloves. I never did get a look at her face or her hair, but she had a beautiful figure. Not as big as a fourteen even. But still," Beatrice said, and frowned.

"Still?"

"I didn't just get the feeling she was young. I couldn't tell you why, either. Just a—maybe a kind of—the way she carried her shoulders, and maybe the way she put her hand on his arm when they were getting into the car. You know? A kind of—"

"Practiced?" Jane asked. "As if she had a well-used set of tricks?"

"That's just exactly it," Beatrice said with relief. She got up and took her plate to the sink. "I felt kind of dirty in this house ever since. He didn't have a right to use his mother's house that way."

Jane carried her cup over. "I don't suppose she dropped a lace handkerchief with her name embroidered in the corner," she said, "so you'd know who she was?"

"She didn't drop a thing," Beatrice said, coloring again. "I went in Steven's room to look. It was neat as a pin, bed smooth and all made up tidy, no powder on the dresser, no hairs, no pins, no nothing. Nothing in the scrap basket. Steven was awful careful. Maybe that's why he was so neat—he'd got used pretty early to leaving no tracks."

Jane stood looking at the big girl. "I wouldn't be surprised if you had something there, my girl," she said. "I wouldn't be surprised at all."

Mrs. Graham's buzzer sounded twice. That meant breakfast in ten minutes.

ELEVEN

Matthew said, "Turn right at the next corner, Helen. This is Burke's place coming up. There it is. The house on the right. He'll be expecting us. I told him we were coming."

"That was bright," Helen commended. "Gives him a chance to get his expression adjusted. After all…"

Matthew said, "He's a good guy, Helen. After all— if you will allow me to finish it—you are an innocent woman. The court said so."

Helen did not answer. Coming into the well-kept town of Mapleton, its pleasant homes set in orderly and tended gardens, she had had a moment of panic. If she came here, she would live under her own name. That was part of the plan. She would be Helen Graham, the woman who was still strongly suspected of killing her husband.

She followed Matthew up the walk to the house, admiring it. The Pattersons must be very comfortable. The house was one of the modern ranch types, compact and neat. A breezeway at one end separated it from an obvious studio; the whole north wall was a plate-glass window and there was a skylight set into the sloping roof.

Matthew stepped to the stone slab at the front door

and rang the bell. There were immediate vigorous foot-steps somewhere inside, and the door was opened wide. Helen had not thought particularly what this artist friend of Matthew's would be like; she knew few artists, and it was always impossible to predict Matthew's friends anyway. If she had formed a mental picture it was of a rather weedy middle-aged male, with spindly muscles and a straggling haircut.

Burke Patterson was bigger than Steven had been. He was probably thirty-five, no more, and he had thick blond hair that was supposed to be slicked down but which stood up in an absurd cowlick at the crown of his head. His eyes were gray and smiling and he had a deep warm voice that was full of friendliness. He said warmly, "Well, Matthew, my friend, it's darn nice to see you. Come in." He shook hands with Matthew as if they really were friends. Matthew said, "My sister-in-law, Burke, Helen Graham."

He held out his hand, and she put her own in it. "How do you do," she said, and stood looking at him. He was examining her face as if he had never seen a face before. Probably the artist's compulsion. He said nothing. Helen heard herself fumbling with words. "It's good of you to let us come."

He said, "Yes," as if he hadn't heard her. He dropped her hand, and then touched her elbow lightly to turn her toward a living room visible beyond the hall. Matthew had gone on. For a moment she and Burke Patterson were alone in the hall, and a mirror at the end caught them as they stood together. Helen got a sudden very strange feeling, as if she were looking at an old familiar picture.

"Come and sit down," he said. "I'll get a drink."

Helen said confusedly, "I hope this won't disturb your wife's plans, our coming so unceremoniously."

He turned and stared at her in something like

astonishment. He said, "*I* haven't got a wife," as if it were something she should have known.

"Well, sorry," Helen said. She sat down in the leather chair he indicated and her eyes took in the general masculinity and disorder of the room. No, he very obviously didn't have a wife, this large young man who looked as if he grew apples or operated a fishing schooner for a living, instead of producing the really exquisite three-dimensional illustrations with their subtle colors that were in all the leading magazines. He was still staring at her, standing in front of a tremendous homespun-covered sofa, whose slip cover was on crooked and even a little torn at the hem. From underneath it two large mashed-down bedroom slippers protruded. There was no rug of any size on the floor, only three or four cotton scatter rugs, too small, not related to each other. The tables were piled with books and magazines and ash trays, the mantel over the really nice stone fireplace was a repository for any number of drawings, cards, cigarette boxes, more ash trays, and a large emerald-green Buddha who deserved a better fate than to be the centre of such an untidy muddle.

Burke said to Helen directly, "Are you really the girl who was tried for murder?"

"Yes."

"For God's sake," he said bitterly. He went across the hall and came back with a large tray holding bottles and glasses. He set it down on top of a pile of magazines on the biggest table. "You be bartender," he told Matthew. "I'll have beer." He sat down in his chair again and went back to looking at Helen. "What started that? Who had that bright idea?" he demanded.

Helen felt her heart warming toward him. It was as if a clean wind had blown across her, as if in it she could smell spring. She found herself almost smiling. She said, "It sounded all right to a number of people at the time."

"Nuts," he said rudely.

There was a heavy padding sound at the door. Without looking, Burke shouted, "Well, come in." The latch lifted, and into the hallway came the largest dog Helen had ever seen. He was a great Dane, a tremendous beast, sleek and tawny like a lion, but with a gentle face and sad, weary, resigned eyes. He stood for a moment surveying everyone and then came on into the room. "It's King," Burke said. "He's harmless. He's very deceptive. He's made of very soft butter. His favorite playmate is the two-month-old kitten who lives behind us. He carries it around in his mouth. It's about half as big as his foot."

"Hello, King," Helen said agreeably. He came over to her and looked directly into her face. He sniffed and lay down beside her. It was slightly like having a freight train coming to sit in the front garden.

Burke said, "You like dogs?"

"I never had anything to do with this much dog. You ought to get a chihuahua. Contrast."

"That's an idea. He'd love it. It's a darn good idea. King is a very lonesome dog. He suffers. Sometimes when I'm trying to paint he lies on the floor suffering until I have to quit and go for a walk or something with him. He's a darn nuisance."

King looked at his master and blinked serenely.

"He must eat an *awful* lot."

"Keeps me poor," Burke said cheerfully. "What are you having to drink, or does Matthew know?"

"Nothing right now, thank you."

He took his beer and sat down again. Matthew, sipping comfortably at his glass, asked him something about a mutual acquaintance of times past and they discussed people. Helen shook herself mentally and got herself adjusted. She had certainly not been prepared for Burke Patterson or anything remotely like him.

He finished the conversation with Matthew and

came back to her. "Matthew says you're interested in coming out here to live?"

"I don't know. I have a small son. He's at school. I want him to be with me. We haven't a house. So... Mapleton sounded attractive." She thought, "I don't like to be devious with this man, but I must." She said, "The town looks very nice. What are the people like?"

"Just like people everywhere, only maybe a little more so. We get along very well, I think. Just big enough, just close enough to the city so we don't get bogged down in ourselves. Matter of fact, it's a swell place to live."

She said slowly, her eyes on his, "Would I be wanted?"

He thought about that. He knew what she meant. He said, "I can't think of a better Ontario community for you to come to. People are fairly intelligent, fairly sophisticated. There'd have to be a small time of adjustment. No use pretending otherwise. But they'd soon see how wild all the ideas were."

Matthew said soberly, "It was mostly my mother's fault, Burke. She was so disturbed at the thought of—well, of suicide. She forced the police's hand."

Burke's blond eyebrows went up. He said to Helen, "You bitter about that?"

"Not very. I just—" She stopped. Looking at him, she had an odd idea that he knew what she had done, and that he didn't like it. To give up bitterness, resentment, was to bury oneself, somehow; to stop being proud, maybe to stop living a little. She wasn't quite sure about some point along in there; maybe you were humble and you were just pretending, even to yourself. Maybe that was true, Helen thought suddenly, and buried that too.

She went back to her pattern. She said, "I've heard that the country club out here is very nice."

"It's a real community center. We do everything out there from little theatre to lawn bowling. Never seen it?"

"No. I'd…like to."

"There isn't anything stopping us," he said. "Let's take a run out there now, look the place over, look the town over…I can point out a few possibles for you in the way of houses. As a matter of fact, there's one on the next lot, new, just being finished. You've got a lot of money, haven't you?"

Matthew choked on his drink. Helen said serenely, "There might be quite a good deal."

"I haven't got any money, but I earn all I want. And painting isn't like some other jobs. You never retire. You get better and richer as you get older, like Grandma Moses." He got up. "Come on, Matthew, down the hatch. We can get a refill out at the club. King, we're going to the club. You want to come?"

King opened an eye and looked thoughtfully at his master. He considered. Then he began to get up, in sections, one huge leg and then another, the rear section last. "Can he ride in your car?" Burke inquired. "No… it's a coupé. I'll get mine out."

When he was gone Matthew said carefully, "Well, what do you think of him?"

"Is he as honest as he sounds?"

"Just exactly."

"I think he's one of the nicest people I ever knew."

"There's something wrong with him, though."

"What?"

"He's a woman hater."

"He doesn't act like one."

"He isn't married. He doesn't—I mean to say, it doesn't seem—he brushes them off," Matthew said rather confusedly. "He likes women as people. He doesn't like them as women."

"Well," Helen said calmly, "that's fine with me. Nothing could be better, far as I'm concerned."

TWELVE

They sat in the large oak-raftered room at the Mapleton Country Club for a long time, looking out over the greens of the golf course, turning now at the end of April into smooth emerald stretches, already enticing some people in spite of the chilly wind and the hint of rain in the air. There were a few youngsters out on the tennis court too, hearty teen-agers, and there were obviously other games going on elsewhere, judging from the number of people of all ages who came in and out of the clubroom. At one table in the corner four women had been sitting ever since Helen and Burke and Matthew had come in, and at sight of them, in a corner that was a little dim, Helen's heart had moved quickly. But now she had crossed them all off. There was no small fair woman with them, vivacious, animated, with a beautiful figure.

Other women had come in and out of the room all afternoon, and Helen had looked them over carefully, but the description fitted none of them. There were plenty of men coming and going, most of them young; there were two or three groups of middle-aged men around, and one table out on the glassed-in terrace was the site of a bridge game between four octogenarians.

"How do you like it?" Burke inquired.

"It looks wonderful. Everybody from Grandpa to the babies. Well…not really babies. I haven't seen any children as young as my Jamie."

"Wait till summer. The swimming pool is what gets them. There's a big Jungle Gym out back, below the hill. You wade through infants all summer long. King has a delectable time. He lies down in the middle of the whole tangle of them and they crawl in his ears and hang around his neck. I did a couple of pieces, a black-and-white drawing and a cover. They were well received," he said modestly, and grinned at her.

"I'm sure they were."

A pair of beautiful youngsters came in the door and climbed on the stools before the counter. They were about fifteen, a boy and a girl, obviously brother and sister, obviously twins. Burke's eyes followed hers. "Aren't they something?" he said. They both had crisp silky gilt hair curling all over their heads, and dark eyes. They were small-boned and elegantly fastened together.

"Have you painted them?"

"Not yet. I'm going to this summer. The—well—" he stopped. He got out his pipe and filled it from a green oilskin pouch. "The girl's going to be a beauty," he said, although it was not the sentence he had begun. "The boy too, probably, but I hope he toughens up some. He looks too much like a girl yet."

A man came into the room and went directly to the two children. He climbed up on the empty stool between them and all three sat having Cokes.

"Not their father?" Helen murmured, looking at his stolid thickset body, the round bald head edged with a fringe of sparse graying hair.

"Yes. Name's Martin. Harry Martin. He's crazy about the kids. Can't do too much for them."

As if Martin had heard his name, he turned and looked straight across at Burke, who raised a hand amiably. At that moment the boy and girl scrambled down and started for the door. Martin called after them in a heavy voice, "Don't be more than another half hour, then. I'll wait on the porch." He got down from the stool. Burke turned. He said, "Hey, Harry…who owns that cottage on the lot right back of you, beside me? Is it still the builder? I heard he'd sold it to some real estate company."

Martin stopped. He had rather a flat face, eyes set into it flatly. "You want to buy it?"

"Just asking."

"Well, the builder's still got it, Burke. He wants

fourteen thousand. Seems like an awful lot for such a small place. But it's made of good stuff." He looked at Helen again, with some curiosity in his glance, then moved off. Matthew, out on the terrace, sitting alone at the railing looking over the gardens, got up with his empty glass and turned toward the door. Helen said quickly, "I think we'd likely better go." She got up. Burke followed her. She went to Matthew and walked along beside him briskly toward the far door and the drive. "We have to go home," she said.

"I dunno why," Matthew replied. "I was just going to get another drink."

"Have one at my place," Burke interposed. "I want to show your sister-in-law my etchings, anyway."

"Oh well, all right," Matthew said amiably enough, and got into the car without further protest.

"Where's King?"

"He probably went home. Or he may be waiting around for Don and Dorothy Martin. It's their kitten who's won his heart, the old dope."

"Have you painted that? The kitten and the big dog?"

"No, and I guess I better. It's always sure-fire."

At his door she said, "We mustn't stay a minute. Only—is that the cottage, on the other side of your place?"

"Yes—beyond the lilac trees. You ought to have a look. It's on a very big lot, so you could add to it if you liked. Do you do anything? Write, paint, sculpt, weave? You'd need some kind of a workroom."

"No, not yet. Maybe I'll take up something."

"Let's trot over and see if it's unlocked," he said. "It likely is. Nobody locks anything in Mapleton. You hear a noise in the kitchen in the middle of the night and it's the neighbors come to borrow eggs for their breakfast. Cozy." He settled Matthew in the living room again and came back. He took Helen's elbow and they went out and down the quarter block of street.

The new house was a Cape Cod cottage, white clapboard, with wide windows and a beautiful door. It was set on a lot at least two hundred feet wide. "It's a darling," Helen said.

"You like houses?"

"I think I could get very fond of houses. I've never lived in one I liked much, or in one of my own. I don't know anything about them."

"What'd you take in college?"

"You mean, I don't seem to know anything?" She found herself smiling up at him. "I took Honors English. I was going to teach. My father's subject is English and I like it very much. I did teach for a year."

"Ever try to write?"

"Now look," Helen said. "I have no talents. I am a very simple person, non-creative, non-complicated. I live from one day to the next without much fever, if you know what I mean."

He opened the door of the little house. "You mean, you could live that way," he said, and his voice echoed in the empty rooms.

It was a simple house, nicely proportioned. A living room occupied the whole eastern end, a dining room and kitchen the west. There was a washroom at the end of the downstairs hall, three bedrooms and a bathroom above. It was a dear little house. It wouldn't have done for Steven at all, but it looked just about right for her and Jamie.

Going back to Burke's house, she was suddenly tempted to ask him outright about the woman. If she described her, knowing her as she knew her now, pink curtains, red negligee, fluttery hands, manner, he would know who she was, if she lived in Mapleton. She fought down the temptation.

Matthew had fallen asleep on the sofa. Burke said, "Let him sleep, poor guy. Come on and take a look at the studio. You might even like some of my stuff." On the way through the breezeway he said, "Is he drinking like this all the time?"

"Pretty much."

"He's kind of all right, too, you know. Always was. But he never had a hope. That woman—his mother—he was always like a tiny little nut in a great big shell. Might have been a good enough nut if she'd paid any attention to what kind it was." He opened the studio door. "Women have a lot to answer for," he said grimly. He turned on the light.

A huge oil on the end wall sprang into immediate brilliance. It was a painting of a woman. She was small and fair and she had floating silky hair.

She was dressed in a clinging robe of dark blue velvet. Her face was turned away and she stood with a rose at her lips. She had a waist that a man's two hands could span, and high, firm, lovely breasts.

Burke was moving round the room, intent on getting something to show her. Helen said in a low flat voice, "Who is that?"

He turned and caught her line of vision. He said coldly, "Oh, just one of the neighbors. She poses for me a good deal."

"What's her name?"

He looked at her sharply.

"She's—she's beautiful," Helen explained. "I wondered…"

He said judiciously, "It's about as beautiful a body as a woman could hope to have."

"A woman? Not a—a girl?"

"It's Donna Martin," he said. "You saw her husband this afternoon. The man who came over to our table. Those twin youngsters are hers. She looks like a girl…I turned her face away. Even that's not so old. But…she's forty, I imagine. She looks about twenty-five if you're not in too good light. Her husband…he's older again."

After a minute Helen said, "I see." She turned away from the painting with an effort. She said calmly, "And now, where are these etchings, Mr. Patterson?"

THIRTEEN

Jerry said, "What do you want me to do with stuff like Steven's golf clubs?"

Helen, seated at Steven's desk in the room that he had called his study, glanced up from the papers in her hand. Jerry had his sleeves rolled up and was emptying the clothes closet. On the floor at his feet was Steven's leather Gladstone, filled now with small personal effects; Steven's pipes, his two silver cups won long ago at college for athletic proficiency, his camera, all the things it might be good to give Jamie someday as mementos of the father he would have forgotten. But the golf clubs?

"What do people do with them, Jerry? Do you want them?"

"Won't be playing much golf," Jerry said coldly. He regarded the clubs, as he did everything of Steven's, with an unadmiring eye.

"Don't you know some young man at University who could do with being outfitted? Poor but promising, and needing these items to round out his life?"

"It's an idea," Jerry said thoughtfully. "Sure. I'll pack them all up together and then ask around the fraternity. There'll be somebody, or a few somebodies. Steven sure had the equipment, even if he didn't use it much."

Helen went back to the letter she had been studying. It was from her lawyer, an informal document accompanied by a sheaf of careful-looking reports.

The accountant who has made this survey is one of the best available. His reports can be trusted implicitly.

It appears that Mr. Steven Graham's affairs were in excellent condition. His initial success, his first money, came about through his having bought, on some private information, a hundred shares of an oil stock when it was practically worthless. Almost at once it skyrocketed and he had a sizable paper profit. He then went in person to Edmonton and there, using his new and lucky money, bought ten acres of farmland on the far edge of a tract as yet only suspected of being oil-producing. Within two months a gusher came in about four miles away, and at once the territory was covered with people attempting to buy in on it. Mr. Graham was one of the fortunate in that he had the oil and mineral rights; and he was offered fabulous sums for it but refused to sell. Oil was discovered next door to him, and at this point he entered into a thoroughly legitimate deal which brought him a large down payment and a share of profits which is being regularly paid. The remainder of his money has come through buying and selling stocks. There is no hint of anything wrong. The word in the brokerage houses is that he was a "natural" for luck.

Helen put a hand to her forehead and propped it as she considered. The report went on.

Mr. Graham's affairs were astonishingly well documented. His bank deposits, his broker's invoices and reports, his deeds and leases, including those in your name, are in perfect order. There seems to be nothing missing from the record, and the final word is that only probate of your husband's will is now necessary to put into your possession, without any encumbrances or difficulty, his very large estate.

She laid the paper down. A half million dollars. Her father's salary had never been more than five thousand. Jerry, in the research lab, would get about eighteen hundred this coming year. These were sums she understood. When she had taught, her own earnings had been twenty-eight hundred dollars for a year. These were reasonable amounts of money, on which you could afford certain types of clothes, go to certain places on holiday, places like rented cottages in Muskoka, or, if you saved, take a boat trip up the Saguenay or a motor trip around the Gaspé.

"Jerry."

He stood up, red-faced, with a pair of oiled fishing boots. "Away at the back," he grunted. "Swell boots." He rubbed his nose with the back of his hand. "What do you want?"

"Am I a simple honest soul?"

He grinned at her. "Kind of," he admitted. "What'sa matter, you getting a yen for glamour?"

She got up and went to the mirrored door of the bathroom opening from this study. She inspected herself carefully. She had her mother's good bones, that was one thing. She said, "It's not exactly glamour. I feel terribly humdrum. I can't sculpt or weave or write or paint or even make roses out of pink crepe paper. I am very uncomplicated and uninteresting."

Jerry dropped the boots. He sprawled down in an armchair and got out his cigarettes. His eyes were on her face. "You know what I always thought?" he said finally.

"What?"

"Well, what chance did you have to be *anything*, yourself, married to that one? If you wanted to keep things straight, you had to spend your whole time at it, watching and weighing. Probably afraid that if you let yourself go the least bit you'd be taking the lid off something, God knows what. That's what you always acted like, these last few years anyway."

"I guess people can develop. Only I don't feel very talented. Maybe I could start a used-Christmas-card exchange, or something. Would that be creative?"

Jerry eyed her. "Does everybody have to be creative? Can't a few people just sort of fill the gaps, I mean, keep life going on serene and smooth for the rest? I like the idea. Me, I'm going to marry a girl as near like you as I can find, only I'd like her to laugh more."

"Well, thanks, pal," Helen said, and felt the warmth in her cheeks. She went back to Steven's desk. She put the report carefully back in its envelope and laid it to one side. She bent and began opening the drawers of the desk, taking every scrap of paper out of each one and piling it on the surface.

Jerry finished his cigarette and went back to his sorting. He dragged a number of items out and carried them in armfuls to the living room, sweaters and ski pants, evening clothes and a whole baker's dozen of Steven's jaunty hats.

Helen sorted the pile of papers before her carefully. There was not much miscellany in Steven's desk, as might have been expected. All the papers relating to investments and income were gone, had never been in this desk, but in the filing cabinet beside it. The filing cabinet was empty and the papers with the lawyer.

The desk had held such things as personal bills for taxis, motorcar service, tailor's accounts, club statements, odds and ends of personal letters. Steven's pockets had all been most carefully emptied and the findings brought here. If there was anything on record to prove the identity of the woman in his life, who had bought the red gown, occupied his apartment, who had seen and perhaps handled the sedative bottle in that other apartment bathroom, it would be here.

Helen saw again the painting in Burke Patterson's studio, and caught again the self-consciousness in his voice as he had spoken of the woman in the painting. A fresh scene, a new slant on the woman, was building itself into Helen's mind. Was she a *femme fatale*? Was she the older woman who, because of her obvious experience, her skilled charm, her carefully tended beauty, often had a great fascination for younger men? It might be, Helen thought, that such a woman might present a deep challenge to those less sophisticated; to the Burkes as well as the Stevens. She did not like the thought; and after all, Burke was no youngster. He was an open sort of person, however, and it might be that the guarded, the hidden life of the woman would have created in him a dark interest. It might be, of course, that…well, that he had been, was, in love with her. He had a dozen paintings of her, all different, done over a period of years; nearly all with her face turned away, not one a direct recognizable portrait of a countenance. But the body, the poses, the hands, the very being of the woman lay open on the canvas for all to see and attempt to read. She fascinated the artist; what she did to the man…

Donna Martin.

The bills were piled carefully at the left. Helen took each one up and read it carefully, making sure it was what it appeared to be. She got through the major portion of the papers fairly quickly, and there was nothing that should not have been there. In the easy collection of any other man, surely there would have been something unguarded, ticket stubs, the wrong letter, even a note treasured and forgotten. There was nothing. Helen turned each piece of paper over and scanned the back, she opened every fold, and nowhere was there a single word that would give any evidence as to the existence of Donna Martin. Yet it was in this desk that the sheaf of canceled checks signed H. Brown had been found; so he had thought it a secure place. If anything existed it had to be here.

She opened the brown folder which held the personal letters and went through it carefully. There were very few; Steven had always been good at destroying them. There was one from somebody who signed himself Dick, thanking Steven effusively for a loan which he had apparently had at Christmas; there were a few invitations, dated early in January, just before Steven's death and obviously unanswered, since Steven's meticulous pencil had not ticked them off. There was a request that he serve on the board of the golf club, a notification that his luncheon club membership was being renewed for the coming year, and a letter from a leading distillery asking for his endorsement of their product.

She had dropped all the letters back into the file and was on her feet, to go and lay it in the fireplace with other things to be burned, when she realized that something had caught at her mind. It was a photographic mind. The eyes took a picture of something and much later the mind took over, to inspect the picture at its leisure. Now she realized that she had seen something that was wrong. Not the name of Donna Martin, as she had half expected, but something else, something less pertinent and yet odd. She opened the brown folder and laid it flat on the desk. She went over its contents again, slowly, word by word.

Jerry came back into the room. He said, "I got an idea...don't you think all these clothes and this stuff of Steven's ought to go to Matthew?"

Helen paused with her finger on a page. She said

absently, "He's got a complete outfit of anything he wants, Jerry. He doesn't get around much in the circles Steven moved in. He'd just take them to a secondhand store and sell them for liquor money."

"Sure, I guess so," Jerry said. "I was just trying to be fair."

He took down another armload of clothes and carried them out to the living room. Helen turned back to the papers.

The thing she had seen was in the letter from the distillers. It was on a beautiful gold-embossed letterhead. It said:

> *Dear Sir:*
>
> *For years we have valued you as one of our most distinguished customers. Your continued patronage has been a source of satisfaction to us, as you know.*
>
> *May we now ask your opinion? We are developing a totally new idea, beginning a new venture with our company, and we very much want the advice of our trusted and well-informed customers. We are therefore sending you some pamphlets containing information and samples of our new products, and should be most grateful for your true reaction.*
>
> *Sincerely yours,*
>
> *J. V. Milgrim and Co.*

Now that looked all right, Helen told herself. What had troubled her?

There were no pamphlets here.

She did not remember any samples of Milgrim's products coming into the house. She had heard of those samples...men who got a case of choice whiskey at Christmas or even on their birthdays, if they were important enough, and so, with all their friends, became firm customers for all the years. There had been no gift case of whiskey come to this house. Such a sizeable thing she would have had to know about. There had been nothing. And Steven had no other address...no legitimate address.

What her mind had seized on, she realized abruptly, was the date. It was January 19...of the *previous* year.

That was surely very odd. There was nothing in this file, in this desk, dated earlier than December of that year. Nothing had been kept for almost a whole year—and why should one letter—this letter—have been overlooked?

Had the whiskey come last year? She could not remember, but she did not think so. It was the sort of thing Steven bragged about, the attention he got from all sorts of sources now that his name was important. After years of inferiority he was suddenly somebody, and he gloried in it.

She sat and stared at the letter.

A case of whiskey?

The letter did not mention anything so bulky as a case of whisky. It did not mention anything specific except...a new product. A new development.

Wit the letter in her hand, she got up and went to the kitchen. She opened the cupboard door and took down the little red bottle on the top shelf. She inspected the label carefully. It was an importation, or appeared to be, from Mexico—tequila. It had nothing at all to do with Milgrim's. How could it have?

But after a time she carried bottle and letter back to the study and put them into a brown envelope together and sealed the envelope. She took it and put it into her own case in her bedroom.

FOURTEEN

It was the first day of June, and in the bedroom of her house on Shore Street in Mapleton, Donna Martin was trying on the summer dress her mother had just finished. The mate to the dress, finished and lying on the bed, was for Dorothy. They had worn mother-and-daughter matching dresses for years, ever since the fashion started, and it was really, Donna always thought, awfully cute. Years ago, when Dorothy had been just a little thing, six and eight and even ten, people had always said, "Oh, how wonderful! Another little Donna, a real miniature!" And now they said, "If you two aren't exactly like sisters! Nobody could possibly tell you apart, when you wear those darling poke bonnets that match your dresses."

Donna looked at herself intently in the long cheval glass, swinging on its big mahogany frame. She reached out and straightened the mirror, tightening the screw at the side to hold it. Her fingers went to the fine narrow ruffle edging the square neck of the dress. She said, "Mamma, are you sure it isn't too—well, just a little too young?"

Over her shoulder, her mother's eyes met hers in the glass, and she thought, as she had a million times before, how awful it would be to look like her mother. Her own face there in the glass was small, with a pointed chin and delicate nose and lovely delicate rose-flushed skin. Her mother's was worn and old, without much shape at all, a good deal the color of a beige doeskin glove that had been worn and washed too often. Her eyes were pale and her thick lips a sort of bluish gray. Her teeth didn't fit too well, either, and sometimes they clicked when she talked. They clicked now, and she did the ugly thing with her tongue that pushed them back in. Then she said, "It isn't a bit too young. Why shouldn't you wear pretty young things when you've got the figure for it? People enjoy looking at you, so bright and fresh and pretty. I don't know how many times they tell me how pretty you look."

"Well," Donna said. She touched her hand to the loose springing tendrils of hair at her temple. She settled the dress over her hips. Nylon, it was, pale pink with a fine white silky thread woven into it. "I like the skirt," she decided. "It hangs beautifully, Mamma."

"Well, it's real easy to make a thing hang nice on a nice figure. So I can't take much credit."

"Where is Dorothy? She ought to be home dressing."

"I'm just as glad she isn't. I've got another two feet of hem to do. She said there wasn't any hurry, it's only over to the Kendertons'. She's over there anyway, helping them get the barbecue set up."

"She'll come home filthy," Donna said. She gave a last look at herself in the mirror and then crossed the room to the window. This room, her mother's room, was at the back of the house, and the windows looked into their own back garden, then over the back garden of the new cottage immediately behind them, diagonally into Burke's place, and past him, across the street, to the rambling old house and grounds of the Kendertons. The children were all over there, milling around in the garden. It wasn't going to be much of a party, nothing exciting...Just the neighbors, really, in to meet Betty's sister from California. All very straighforward and respectable, mothers and fathers and children out in the garden, the fathers talking about the coming golf season, the mothers exclaiming over the first iris in Betty's flower-show collection, the children stuffing themselves with Betty's barbecued spareribs and potato chips out of big wooden bowls, and probably rhubarb short-cake with thick globs of whipped cream for dessert later.

Behind her, her mother murmured, "Harry said he'd be home early. He said he thought he'd leave the office about four."

"Oh, he'll get away early, all right, for a backyard kid party," Donna said flatly. "Make it a real do, cocktails out at Lady Burnside's, with everybody that *is* anybody there from Toronto, and what does he do? Gets home at half past six, just barely time to catch the party as it's breaking up. And even then stands around all sweaty-looking and red-faced, as if he was the garbage collector, or somebody."

Her mother drew a long breath. "Harry's a real good man," she said as automatically as she had been saying it for years. "He's as good to you as he can be, dear, and he'll do anything for the children. He's a good provider and a kind father, and there's lots worse."

"Sure, sure," Donna said impatiently, "and I married him at seventeen, one of the years he was in the money, and he bought me a big diamond and took me to Bermuda and I thought life was going to be a bed of roses."

"You was nearer twenty, Donna, and pretty dis-satisfied with the boys that hung around. You know that. I used to try to tell you maybe Harry wasn't just right for you, fifteen years older and not very handsome. But you thought he was just right."

"Oh, don't start that again," Donna said coldly. She pushed up the window and put her hands on the sill to lean out.

A big moving van was turning the corner in front of Burke's house and moving along the street. Donna watched it, not really thinking about it. Her mind was on Burke. He would be at the Kendertons' party, and if she watched her opportunity she might get a chance to say exactly the right word to him today. He would be taken with this pink dress. It had the kind of shimmeriness to the fabric that was a challenge to his painter's hand, and he liked these soft, very full skirts. Maybe it would strike just the right note with him. It wasn't like the clothes she'd worn all winter, either. Harry would like it. He didn't like severe little black dresses worn with one enormous emerald clip (you could get such a clip for about three dollars at a costume-jewelry place, she'd told him, but he still didn't like it) or a stark white draped jersey evening dress with a modest-looking high-necked top and no back at all. Her mother was such a good dressmaker that she could manage sophistication as well as the ingénue type, but the way Harry carried on about them spoiled everything. Harry wanted his wife to be sweet, simple, unspoiled, innocent, with her eyes always modestly downcast. A rope tied around her wrist, too, Donna thought coldly, and him holding the other end of it.

The moving van stopped at the new cottage right behind their house. Over the tops of the tall syringa bushes, heavy now with sweet-smelling white blossom, Donna saw it lurch into the new driveway and edge itself up to the back door of the house. Men got out and one of them unlocked the door.

"Well!" she told her mother. "The cottage must have been sold. I didn't hear anything about it."

With Dorothy's dress in her arms, her mother got up to come and peer out. "People moving in, anyway," she said. "Wonder who they are? It'll seem queer to have a family in here, always been an empty lot before."

Donna watched the men slide a sofa out of the truck. "Looks like new furniture, the way it's wrapped up. Maybe they're newlyweds." She drew a long breath. "I hope they're nice and have some life to them," she said. "I certainly hope they are."

"Well, so do I," her mother agreed. "You need some new company." She shook the dress and put it on a hanger. "There, it's ready. Now, if she just comes home to put it on…"

"Do you think she might not?" Donna asked sharply.

"Well, she said it seemed kind of a waste of time.

She's been over there all afternoon anyway, and she said it looked silly to come home and get all dressed up and walk back just to make an entrance."

"Oh, that child is a nuisance," Donna decided. "What's she got on today?"

"Her old blue jeans and a T-shirt. She's got her hair in pigtails and she looks about ten years old," her mother said dryly. "She's not dressed for a party."

Donna stood with her eyes on her mother, but her mind was going over and over the party. Maybe this was better. Let Dorothy stay in her jeans and shirt and look ten years old.

She said casually, "It's nearly five. Harry ought to be along any minute. I think I'll go over to the Kendertons'. Maybe I'll send Dorothy home to get dressed." She eyed her mother speculatively. She said, "Don't you really want to come? Betty Kenderton asked you."

"No, no, I don't want to go. I don't know what to talk about to people like that. The talk goes on all around my head and I feel silly. They don't care anything about me, and I know it, and that's fine. I'd rather stay here and get myself a quiet supper down in the kitchen and do up the rest of the ironing. My feet hurts some, anyway, and it isn't my idea of being comfortable, hobbling around on the uneven ground and having a flock of youngsters pushing and shoving and yelling all over me."

"It isn't mine, either," Donna said. "I see your point, Mamma. But don't work too hard."

She went downstairs and out the side door, to emerge on the street leading to Burke's corner. She walked slowly along past the flowering hawthorn and the green hedge on Burke's property. He was not in sight. He might be in the house, but he was more likely in the studio, and it wouldn't do to go and see. The studio had no outside door; it was reached only through the enclosed breezeway from the house. Nobody ever tried to find Burke there; he hated being interrupted when he was working. She glanced at his house to see if she could catch a glimpse of him inside the place; you could see almost the whole interior through the picture windows. He was not in sight.

She crossed the street slowly, admiring the toes of her white nylon lace sandals. She went in through the Kendertons' gate and up the walk to the house. The door was open; the whole house was open and empty, and they were all in the back garden. She walked through the house, casting a swift glance at Betty Kenderton's modern furniture, at the over-all broadloom on the floor, the grand piano in the corner of the living room. The room seemed even bigger because of the five-foot-square mirror hung over the outsize chesterfield. Donna stopped for a moment to look at herself in the mirror against the moss green of Betty's curtains. The pink was just right; pale enough to be soft, deep enough to have importance. Not many women could wear pink as she could, nor in this style.

The dining-room door opened on to a flagstone terrace which stretched along the back of the house. From it ran a curved stone walk down into a shallow ravine at the back of the Kenderton garden. There was a tiny stream in the ravine, and Hugh had dammed it up in a series of little pools, and then built his outdoor fireplace nearby.

She paused for a moment at the end of the rock path, on the top of the shallow flight of steps. There were half a dozen people in the hollow, as well as the Kenderton youngsters and Donald and Dorothy. Hugh and Betty, two strangers—that would be Sue and Carter Hill, Betty's sister and her husband—and Burke...well, that was all. Five.

The pink dress caught the eye of Carter Hill. She had never met him. He stood up at once and stared at her. He wasn't bad-looking. Dark, and thin-faced, with very nice California clothes, free and sporty. He had a glass in his hand. The kids stopped making so much noise, just for a second, and Donna heard him say loudly, "Well, look what we've got! A vision in pink, no less."

They all looked at her. Betty, in dark blue sleeveless denim, said calmly, "Hi, Donna, come on in. This is Sue and this is Carter." She got up and went to the fine stone bar Hugh had built along the edge of the stream. "Lemonade as usual?" she asked.

"As usual," Donna said, and went on down to sit beside Hugh on his green bench. She smiled at Sue Carter, a big girl, heavier than Betty, with an orange and black sun dress showing a great deal of tanned back. "It's nice to meet you at last," Donna said in a low voice. Then, "Hello, Burke."

He was leaning against a tree. He regarded her thoughtfully. "Hi," he said.

Carter Hill wasn't so stiff. He was staring at her as she sat against the greenery. He said, "I do believe a rose has just come walking down here from the garden."

Donna glanced at the youngsters, clustering around the stone fireplace. They were all in jeans. She said, "I guess there's no point sending Dorothy home to dress. Unless Elizabeth's going to. Is she, Betty?"

Betty brought the lemonade. She glanced briefly at the children. "It doesn't look as if," she said. "Elizabeth hates clothes, anyway."

Donna thought privately, with good reason, that big hulk of a girl.

Hugh said, "Where's Harry?"

"Oh, he'll be along any minute. He was going to leave the office early. Is that what you did?"

"I didn't go in today. Loafing. Carter and Sue can't stay long so we're concentrating on them." He got up and went over to the barbecue. Donna sat still on the green bench. Burke kept glancing at her.

Harry appeared at the top of the stone steps. He came on down. Hugh turned and yelled at him. "Hi, Harry! Hot in town?" Betty grinned and waved her cooking fork. Burke moved from the tree and went over to a bench near the path, to sit down on it. Sue and Carter were introduced; Betty brought Harry a drink. He took it and then came on to Donna. He dropped down on the bench beside her and put his arm around her for a moment. "You didn't wait for me," he said reproachfully.

"I knew you'd be right along, darling. Did you have a good day in town?"

"Oh, all right. Are you all right? Everything go all right for you? Did you get a good sleep after I left?"

"Just fine. Couldn't be better."

Betty said calmly, "Haven't you been getting enough sleep, Donna?"

Harry said, "She hears every sound in the night. She sleeps like a cat. So she always wakes up tired. I've been making her stay in bed in the mornings." He turned his gaze away from her at last, and said to the others, "I see there's a moving van at the new house. I heard it was sold, but nothing more. They moving in already? Who is it?"

Hugh's red eyebrows went up and he grinned in Burke's direction. Betty laughed. "Ask Burke," she said. "He's the one with the inside information. So far he won't tell."

"Won't tell what?" Harry asked blankly.

"Well, it's like this," Hugh explained, coming over with his glass in his hand. "Somewhere, somehow, Burke's got the inside track on this new neighbor. I heard something about her downtown…a rich young widow, I heard. But Burke knows her."

Donna looked at Burke, startled.

"And *I* saw her," Betty supplied. "Putting two and two together, I remembered that two or three weeks ago I saw Burke showing a girl over the house one Saturday. A very nice-looking girl, tall and dark, with a nice way of holding her head and an easy slow walk. She had a Packard coupé, which sounds sort of rich. So I gather that's our rich young widow, and that Burke is responsible for bringing her into our midst."

Harry said heartily, "Good for Burke. Is it true?" Then, "Oh—would she be the girl you had out at the club one Saturday? I didn't get a real good look at her. But there was something sort of familiar…" He stopped.

Burke said slowly, not in his usual way, "Yes—and I'm not—that is, I showed her the house, yes."

Hugh said, "What's the trouble, Burke? You sorry?"

"No." Burke turned his glass around in his fingers. "She is a very nice person. I've just been wondering…I guess this is it. I guess this is the place and the way to do it."

"To do what?"

"Well…she's got a lot of strikes against her, no matter where she goes to live. I think she's swell. I'm sold on her. I believe in her. But no matter how you look at it, there's bound to be talk. Seems to me if she had a few of us to stand by—sort of sponsor her, start her off on the right foot—it would make things an awful lot easier for her."

Betty said, "Your idea does you credit, my friend. What's the trouble with your rich young widow? She's obviously not maimed or blind, or halt. She looked fine to me. What's the trouble?"

"She's had to…she's been suspected of committing a crime," Burke said.

At his words, something struck deep and hard into Donna's thinking. Not her conscious thinking, but into the place where so much is hidden, spaded over, spread with thick impenetrable moss. She felt herself stiffening.

Hugh's face was interested. Hugh was a lawyer. He said, "What crime? Who is she?"

Burke said strongly, "It'll get said all over the place in the next day or so. Let it. It has to be this way. But... well, she's legally free. And I know she's innocent. The State says so, and as soon as you get to know her, you'll say so too. She's innocent. So I don't think people ought to go tilting at her. Or whatever they do."

Donna couldn't take her eyes from his face. They were all watching him as if he were about to bring a rabbit out of a baby's bonnet. Even Harry sat motionless, fascinated, on the bench.

"Well," Burke said again. "I kind of hate to say her name, to start things. She needs help. She's...the widow of Steven Graham. The crime—" He glanced at Sue and Carter. "She was tried for murdering him. She was acquitted."

There was a long silence. Betty stood staring at Burke. Donna found her eyes going round the company, not daring to look at her own thoughts. Not daring.

Carter said, "They didn't find the real murderer?"

"She was found not guilty and the case was dismissed."

Sue said slowly, "The poor girl. Half the world will always think her guilty."

Burke looked at her gratefully. "That's my point," he said. "That's just exactly my point."

FIFTEEN

It was nine o'clock when they left the Kendertons', Donna and Harry and Burke, and walked across the street together. Donald and Dorothy had gone on ahead, not too pleased to go home while the evening was still bright; but Donna had found herself unable to take the party any longer and the children made a good excuse. "I have to get them to bed," she had explained to the Hills, and had stood up firmly. Harry got up too; he was always anxious to go home.

"Oh, nonsense," Betty said. "They're big enough to get themselves to bed, and anyway, your mother's at home."

Harry came to the rescue. He put his arm around Donna's shoulders and said, "I haven't seen the kids all day, not to speak of. We'd better get them collected up and stowed away. Don! Dorothy! Time for taps, kids."

They came up from the lower ravine, scrambling along in a pack with the Kenderton children. Donna looked narrowly at Dorothy, and the girl's face was pink and laughing. Young Pete Kenderton was hanging on to the end of one of her pigtails, and he had very likely been making some kind of clumsy passes at her. In spite of the jeans and the T-shirt Dorothy didn't look ten years old; her eyes had the beginning of a slanted, almost a flirting look, and her breasts under the clinging knitted cotton were already round and full. Donna thought with a sudden dark anger that here was something else beginning to load her down; this girl would have to be controlled, watched, kept out of trouble.

Dorothy said now, looking at her father, "I don't want to go home yet, Daddy. The evening's just beginning."

"Let's all go down for a Coke," young Pete said in his hoarse voice. It was almost changed, but not always manageable. Donna remembered the boys of her own youth, and their rough urgencies. Pete was almost sixteen and they weren't babies at sixteen, not by any means. She said coldly, "Dorothy's got to come home. Don, take her and go along, right this minute."

Dorothy gave her a flashing quick glance but said

nothing. She pulled away from Pete's clutching hands and ran up the path.

Harry said, "Go along with her, Don."

"Sure," Donald said easily, and to Elizabeth, "See you in the funny paper," and then to Betty, "G'night, Mrs. Kenderton. It was a swell party."

"It *was* a nice party," Donna said sweetly. "I wish you and Carter could stay longer, Sue. Maybe we might run to a party out at the club."

"Well, thanks," Sue muttered vaguely. "If we stay over we'll let you know."

Harry gave Donna a quick look at her words, and she could read his mind. Harry didn't care much about parties at the club. What Harry liked was to stay home with *Time* and *Life* and a good mystery story and have some hot milk about eleven o'clock and then go to bed. And for real fun, what he liked was to help the kids with their homework.

Her mind hadn't really been on a party at the club. As they came out to the street she had looked across to the new cottage, and all the lights were on. There weren't any curtains at the windows yet and the place was like a movie stage, brilliantly lit up.

She said, "Is the—the new neighbor—is she going to stay there now? Is she moved in to stay?"

"Dunno," Burke replied. His eyes were fixed on the cottage too.

Harry said casually, "How'd you get to know her, Burke?"

Donna waited for the answer. Burke said, "Oh, she came out here looking around for a place to live, and her brother-in-law brought her to my place."

"Brother-in-law?"

"Matthew Graham."

Donna said in a low voice, "Is he a friend of yours? I mean—the Graham family…"

"No, I never knew Steven," Burke said shortly. He bent and lifted a stick off the road and carried it along with him. "It's got a nail in it," he muttered. "The kids must've thrown it here."

Harry said, "Why would she pick on Mapleton?"

It was the question Donna had been wild to ask, but hadn't dared. Why would she pick on Mapleton, Steven Graham's widow?

"Don't know, exactly," Burke replied. "She was just looking around, I think, and heard about Mapleton. She's got a young son, kid about six or seven. Wants a house to bring him up in."

Harry said, "What's she like?"

"Well, a nice sensible girl, I'd say. Honest. And seems to me she must have a lot of courage, or she'd run away from all the talk and take the child."

Figures moved suddenly across the lighted windows of the living room in the cottage, a tall girl in a dark dress, and behind her a tall young man. The lights went out. The two people came out of the house and stood at the door, obviously locking it.

"Who's the man?" Harry asked.

"Dunno," Burke said thoughtfully. "Not Matthew, anyway."

"Oh, she'll have friends," Donna heard herself saying. "All that money…she'll have lots of friends."

Neither man answered her. Helen Graham and the young man, down at the other end of the block, walked down the path and got into the Packard coupé sitting there. The young man moved easily. He went round and got into the driver's seat.

"It's her car," Burke said.

Donna took a long breath. "Mapleton is a sort of fashionable place to live. Maybe that's what's brought her here."

"I don't think she cares," Burke said briefly. He

stopped at his corner and turned. "One thing, she knows what she's doing," he said. "G'night."

Harry's fingers on Donna's arm tightened. They walked along the street in silence. He usually had more to say, but Donna was glad of his lack of conversation. Usually he would have made remarks about the rich young widow, and that maybe here was a friend for Donna, someone she could really like at last, not like Betty Kenderton or some of the others. He didn't say a word. He opened the screen door at the side of the house and they went in. Dorothy and Donald were in the kitchen, looking into the refrigerator.

Donna said sharply, "You kids don't need anything more to eat. For goodness' sake, go on to bed."

"Oh, kids always want to eat," Harry said mildly. "I brought out a basket of cherries. Fill a dish and take them upstairs, you two. Don, how's the math? You need any help?"

"No, it's okay," Don said. He lifted out the basket of cherries. "Swell," he said. "Where's a bowl?"

Donna opened the cupboard beside the sink and found an aluminum saucepan. She handed it to Don absently.

"That's my porridge pan for morning," Harry said. "It's the top of the double boiler." He rummaged in the cupboard and came up with a blue bowl. "Take this."

Dorothy said, "Cherries aren't fattening, are they?"

"Never mind about that nonsense," Harry said flatly. His eyes went over her. "You don't need to think about things being fattening."

The children went upstairs, their narrow backs a lot alike in the jeans and cotton shirts. Harry went on standing with his hand on the refrigerator door.

Donna said, "I better go see how Mamma got along with things," and went up the narrow side staircase that led toward her mother's room. Harry didn't answer.

Her mother was in bed, her bulky figure propped against her pillows. She wore a white cotton nightgown, high-necked and with elbow sleeves, and her hair was wound carefully on green rubber curlers. She was reading her Bible, which meant that she was about ready to turn off her light. Donna went into the room and shut the door behind her. She leaned against the door for a minute or so without any life in her.

Her mother said sharply, in a low voice, "Donna! What is it?" She laid the Bible on the square night table.

Donna shook her head warningly. She turned the lock on her mother's door and went across to drop down on the foot of the bed. She said, "You just can't imagine what's happened."

"*What* has happened? You look something awful! What is it? Did Harry…I mean…"

"Mamma, you know who has bought the new cottage? Who's going to live right on my doorstep? I'll have to see her every day, look at her, think about her? You know who?"

"Donna, tell me! Don't get into a state, dear. You'll get all worked up…tell Mamma."

Donna said miserably, "Mrs. Steven Graham, that's who. Mrs. Steven Graham."

Her mother's pale eyes were fixed on her face. Her mother's old hands knitted themselves together. She said in a dull, heavy voice, "That don't make sense."

"It's true."

"But it don't make sense. She don't belong out here. All the places in the world for her to live in…she can't come right on our back doorstep."

"She's come. She's bought the place. She's moving in right now. She's going to bring her little boy. She'll always be there, Mamma, I just can't stand it. Every time I see her, I'll remember…"

After a long time her mother said, "You've got to pull yourself together."

"Don't think I don't know it," Donna said angrily. "The nerve of her! If she knew what she was doing, it couldn't really be much worse. Not even if she knew what she was doing!"

"Donna."

"Yes?"

"Do you think—maybe she *does* know what she's doing?"

"Oh no, no, no! How can she? Anyway, why should she want to? Oh…even if she did know, she couldn't do this! It's terrible. How am I going to bear it?"

"How do you know," her mother said slowly, "how do you know that he didn't tell her about you?"

"Why would he do that? He was *crazy* to keep it quiet. He did everything to make sure nobody could know, and she was the one he didn't want finding it out! If she knew, he said, she would do something. She was already needling him to death about how he got his money, about if he was on the level, and he had to keep a lot of property in her name. If she'd found out about me…oh no, he didn't tell her—and what's more, he didn't let her find out! He was clever, not her. You know he was clever."

"Sometimes wives are cleverer than their husbands think. Sometimes. He might think he had her fooled, but maybe she wasn't. Maybe she's the deep kind."

Donna said bitterly, "Why would she come out here?"

Her mother did not reply. Her face was heavy, full of trouble.

"Oh, if I had it to do over again," Donna said, and stopped. She saw again Steven as he had been that night, only last August, when he had come to the Saturday night dance at the club. Just stopped by, he had said. He'd been with old Mr. Stevenson. They had some kind of deal on. And the old man had brought him to the club for a drink…and the dance was going on…and Steven had seen her dancing. She'd been wearing the new white chiffon. He'd seen her dancing, and he hadn't gone home with Mr. Stevenson. He'd stayed until he met her, until they'd danced together a dozen times. He'd been a wonderful dancer. And right that night she'd felt that life was beginning for her at last. She'd come home and told her mother about it. All the way home, riding beside Harry, full of Steven and the excitement, the glorious wild excitement of having him, so handsome, so rich, of having him turn up like that and fall in love with her. It was the kind of thing a girl hoped for all her life. It hadn't happened to her at the right time, she thought bitterly. Twenty years earlier, it was what she had wanted, hoped for, longed for. Steven was like Prince Charming, handsome and tall and with everything in the world a girl could want. Even to think of Harry now beside Steven made her feel sick, and that night it had been terrible. She had been so aware of the difference between them. She hadn't said a word, she had been even nicer to Harry than usual, although it sickened her. But as soon as she got home she'd had to slip in and tell her mother that something wonderful had happened…and then next day she told her all about it. It wasn't anything she could fight. There was Steven, willing to do anything to be with her, and it was inevitable.

And what would have happened…as time went on? She knew that too. She was sure of him, and had been from the beginning. It was only a matter of giving him time to get on his own feet. He had had his money only a short time, and first there had been his mother, bossing him to death all his life, and then he was tied to Helen. Helen was a cold fish, no wife for a man like Steven. It wouldn't have taken very long to get him to see that—and then a divorce would have been easy. They were already talking about what they'd do…when they could be together always. They hadn't really made plans, but there were ways of doing these things. The wife would likely give him up if she got enough money; she didn't really love him anyway, that was clear enough.

And as for Harry?

Well, she could get around Harry. There had never been a time when he wouldn't give in to her. It would break his heart to do this, because he thought the sun rose and set on her. He always had. But when she made him see that it wasn't a bit of good, that she couldn't and wouldn't live with him any longer, he would give in. He would have to give in; because she would just have gone away with Steven anyway, and Harry would see that he might as well give in. They'd be gone, she and Steven, before she told Harry the score, and by that time he would just have to give in. They'd be in Reno—and they could marry in the States even if Helen and Harry wouldn't consent. They couldn't come back and live in Canada, but who cared about living in Canada anyway? There was all the rest of the world to live in. Reno divorces, American marriage…it would all have been so simple…once Steven got to the point.

"If I had it to do over again," she said, "I'd have worked faster. I guess. What I can't understand, I can never, never understand, is how *he* came to die. Unless—" She stopped. Her eyes went to her mother's face.

"Unless what?"

"Well, Donna said bitterly, "maybe she *is* just too clever. And if she is, then she did kill him after all. And if she killed him…then she knows all about me…and I…"

Her mother said in her slow voice, "The only thing is, you can't get upset. You get upset, and everything falls to pieces. If it isn't an accident, her coming out here, then she's going to be watching you like a hawk. She's going to want to get you upset."

Donna said wildly, "I can't bear it! I can't live this way! I'll go crazy."

Harry's footsteps came along the hall. Like a flash Donna got off the bed. She slipped to the door and unlocked it, noiselessly. She stood with her back against it, her hand on the knob. She pulled herself together with a terrible effort.

Harry rapped at the door. He said, "Mother, is Donna in there? She doesn't seem to be anywhere else."

Donna turned the knob. "I'm here," she said. "I was just telling Mamma about the party. You go along, Harry, I'll come in a minute."

Her mother said evenly, "I want she should take this dress off and leave it here, Harry. There's something wrong with the hem. I won't keep her but a minute."

"Well, all right," he said, and went off satisfied. He went into Donald's room across the hall. Donna heard the rumble of his voice in there.

"You keep yourself pulled together," her mother said under her breath. "Keep pulled together and don't say nothing whatever you do. Don't talk about her to anybody. It'll work out. It's got to work out. Things always does."

SIXTEEN

When Donna had left her room, old Mrs. Corson sat for a long time with her Bible open on her knees, staring at the pages but not seeing them. Donna was in trouble again, and her mother's mind went over and over every aspect of the trouble. It was a terrible thing that no matter what she did, no matter how all her life she had loved the girl and tried to protect her, to shield her, she was always in trouble. Away back twenty years ago, longer than that, twenty-five years ago—back to the time when Donna had been the age Dorothy was now, she had needed so much help. She had been such a pretty girl, always pretty; a beautiful baby, with the silvery curls clustered all over her head, and her eyes even bluer, darker, and more the color of velvet pansies than they were now. She had grown into a real beauty so soon, so early. And her mother, yearning over her, had always been so afraid.

The truth was, of course, that she had not known how far Donna would follow in her father's footsteps.

Thinking of him, of Jake Corson, his wife felt again the old pain and bitterness flood her heart. She had been thirty when she met him, and she had known he was much younger. But he had been beautiful, too, like the pictures of the Greek gods in the schoolbooks, with the white skin and the blond curls, like Donna's, all over his head. She supposed now that she had always known he was worthless. If she hadn't been such a religious girl, so afraid of hell-fire, so anxious to do what was right, maybe she wouldn't have insisted on marrying him. Maybe she would just have let him make love to her and then go on his way. No, she had thought she couldn't bear that; either to be bad herself or to let him leave her. But he had left her; and he had actually meant nothing by marrying her. Marriage was a sacrament to her, a thing built on a promise meant to be kept. For him no promise was meant to be kept. He made one as lightly as another, and was held by none. It was queer that he had hung around her in the first place; she had often thought that. But in every man there was maybe, sometime or another, a need for the security of a pattern, and Jake had found her just when he was in sad trouble and looking for a safe hiding place. She knew that now. The marriage had lasted only a year; and she wasn't even sure that the words said over them at the ceremony had been legal. Donna didn't know how bad he had been. There was no reason for telling her. Just try to keep her out of trouble, that was what had mattered. As far as Donna knew, Jake was dead. He had died when she was a baby and her mother had brought her up by dressmaking, going out to other women's houses and sewing for them, year after year.

It hadn't been much of a life for Donna. She had wanted so much. People had always made a fuss over her and if only she could have had some special chance she could have got to Hollywood, maybe, or at least to New York as a big important model. But it always seemed that something happened to get in her way. If it wasn't one thing, it was another. Once it had looked as if the big gentleman who had the final say was really going to get her into the movies—and then his wife had seen him having lunch with Donna and she had made a lot of trouble. And back in those days Donna had not been doing anything bad. She had known it wasn't smart, that it didn't pay, even if it had been right. You give into a man, her mother had told her over and over, and you're done for, my girl. You'll get nothing out of it but trouble. And Donna had been good—but her mother wondered sometimes now if she wasn't sorry. Because she wasn't satisfied and happy with Harry. She never had been.

It was because she understood how it was with Donna and Harry that she had understood about Steven. Harry had never been handsome. He was kind and good to Donna, because he worshiped her; and he had been wonderful to her mother, always making her welcome in whatever home he could provide at the moment. But nobody could say he was romantic. He knew himself that he wasn't, and when Donna showed signs, as she had fairly often, of liking to dance or flirt a little with other men, he had kept quiet about it. She had never gone very far, her mother was sure of that, until this Steven Graham came along. With him she had been helpless. His pictures in the paper made him out to be real handsome, and Donna said he was. And of course he was so rich, and he knew how to sweep a girl off her feet.

So Steven Graham was dead, and here his widow had come to live right behind them. She didn't know about Donna…did she? How could she? But if she didn't, then how out of all the world had she found this place? And, if she knew anything, how much did she know?

Mrs. Corson got out of bed and went across to the mahogany wardrobe against the inner wall. It was an old-fashioned thing, but she always had liked it. There was a high top shelf above all the clothes hangers, and on it, pushed away back, was the bundle of papers about Steven Graham and what had happened to him. She got the bundle down and took it back to bed with her. She untied the blue strip of cloth holding the bundle— that was flowered seersucker from Dorothy's last-year nightgowns—and looked them over again.

His wife, this girl who had come to live behind them, had been tried for his murder, but they had let her off. She had found his body, and anyway there was a note from Steven about her and how she was bound and determined to get his money. But they couldn't prove that she had given him the dose of stuff that had killed him. It looked as if he'd had some left in a bottle in his medicine cabinet and the druggist said he'd just got that filled the morning he died, but it wasn't open. It still had the druggist's label fastening down the cap, and the druggist had tested it for strength and said it hadn't been opened or watered.

Mrs. Corson looked at the picture of Steven Graham, at the narrow slanted eyes, half laughing; at the good bones in his face, and at the cruel selfish mouth. He was selfish. Donna said the reason he used so much of that stuff was that he had been a heavy drinker and had bad nerves. If he'd been drinking in the daytime and had to go out at night, he'd come home and take a dose of it and sleep like a log for a couple of hours, Donna had said, and then he'd be like new again.

That was what had likely happened the night he died, Donna had said once. He'd come home and had a bath and got into his pajamas and then he'd taken a dose of his stuff so he could have a good nap and be fresh for evening.

He'd been over at the yacht club sitting on the porch with a bunch of his friends, that day he died. And he'd said something to them about having a date for the evening, something he was excited about. But nobody could remember that he'd said what his date was. Nobody.

Had one of the friends kept something back, and told this to Helen? Had one of them known that his date that night was with Donna, that Donna had finally fixed it so that she could get into town to stay all night? She'd never been able to get away for more than an hour or two with him before, an afternoon at the most. But this time she'd been planning to stay all night, because Harry had said he had to go up to Barrie on business and couldn't get back for two days.

And Donna had gone into town, of course, and she had gone up to the apartment and waited and waited for Steven Graham. But he hadn't come; and at two o'clock in the morning she had got a taxi out to Mapleton and come home, angry and crying—but not guessing that Steven was dead and couldn't possibly have kept his date with her. She hadn't known that for a whole day, when the papers came out with his picture on the front page and the headlines.

The wife's picture didn't come out for another day, but by that time it sounded as if they had already suspected her.

Mrs. Corson looked at her picture, the tall dark girl with the serious eyes, and at the little boy, Jamie. Maybe she had had a bad time. She must have had a pretty bad time. But that's what happened to a woman when she married a no-good man; she had to expect to take a lot of bad with the good.

There was a little tapping sound at her door and Mrs. Corson rolled the papers together quickly and went to push them back onto the shelf. It was Dorothy who came in, in the seersucker nightgown, with her long fair hair crinkling down her back. She said, "I didn't think you were asleep. I saw your light."

"You ought to be in bed yourself."

"I know," Dorothy said, still whispering. "What were you doing?"

"Oh, just looking at some old patterns," Mrs. Corson said, and gave the papers another push out of sight. She padded back and got into bed. "Did you get your homework done?"

"I wish everybody didn't always look at me and think homework," Dorothy said indignantly. "Of course I got it done. Gram...have you heard the exciting news? I think I'm kind of scared."

"What exciting news?" Her grandmother watched the bright pretty face, so much like Donna's. Donald's chin was stronger than Dorothy's, and he had ways like his father, but Dorothy was just what her mother had been. "What's so exciting, and do you have to have another new dress for it? I s'pose that's it."

"No, no. This is different. Gram, you know the cottage back of us, the new one—well, you know what? There's a murderess come to live in it!"

Her grandmother drew the pieced quilt up over her. She said at last, "That don't make good sense, child. They don't let murderesses run around loose, you know. Where'd you get that story?"

"Well, the real estate people sold the house to her and then somebody realized who she was...and it was too late. I mean, she paid cash, and so nobody cared. But now they know. Elizabeth and Pete found out this afternoon and told me and Donald. Everybody'll be talking about it tomorrow. Gosh, a murderess..."

"Dorothy, I told you that isn't so. She isn't a murderess. At least…" She stopped.

Dorothy said disappointedly, "Somebody told you about her."

"Your mother heard the news tonight too. She told me. It's a Mrs. Graham. But she's been let go, Dorothy. They couldn't prove she killed her husband. They had to let her go."

"But they didn't prove who *did* kill him, and most people still think she did, Elizabeth and Pete said. She got all the money. Gosh, isn't it exciting, her living right there? She's going to bring her little boy out and live here. It kind of scares me, it's so exciting."

"Well, if I was you," her grandmother said, and stopped again. Maybe this wasn't the way to talk or think. Maybe the best thing that could happen would be to have the woman made so miserable she'd go away again and leave them all alone. Maybe that was what would happen.

"She's awful rich, they say," Dorothy went on, not noticing. "You know, I can hardly believe it. You go along, all bogged down with dumb old homework, and then all of a sudden a murderess moves in next door! Why, it's like a story! I wonder if everybody gets all mixed up in murders without meaning to, just like this? It kind of scares you! As if people could be anybody, if you know what I mean!"

"Maybe nobody really means to get mixed up in it," her grandmother said heavily. "Now go along to bed, child, and let me get some rest. And if I was you…let other people make the trouble. Don't you get mixed up in it. We don't want any part of that kind of trouble. You just keep mum and listen and don't go poking into things that don't concern you."

"Just like an ostrich," Dorothy said. She got up, came over and kissed her grandmother lightly, and went on out to bed.

Mrs. Corson took up her Bible again. She felt very mixed up inside, and not happy. Things didn't happen the way they should.

SEVENTEEN

In the bedroom of his boardinghouse in Mapleton, old Mrs. Denby's rambling comfortable dwelling, P.C. Lake sat writing his report, anxious to set down his facts clearly and exactly for the eyes and mind of Dr. Jonathan Merrill.

As has been previously reported, several short trips were made to Mapleton before the middle of May, trips made for the purpose of discovering if possible the identity of the woman and the man of the Calloran Arms.

It was found best to begin at the country club, and an approach was made in the character of an out-of-work gardener. The club is sufficiently staffed, but the manager is friendly and proved willing to make suggestions as to possible jobs in town. Four days' work was put in as an extra hand at the club, getting the golf course in order. Since most of the workers at the club, both inside and out, are local people, certain information was available. It was also possible during this time to watch all visitors to the club in the hope of seeing either the man or the woman.

Neither was in evidence during that time. But questioning narrowed possibilities down until three or four likely couples could be singled out.

Meanwhile, as you will know, Mrs. Graham came to Mapleton as predicted and bought a certain house on a certain street. It would seem that her own information had led her in certain directions, and our two paths converged. There seems to be little doubt that the woman in the case of Steven Graham is Mrs. Harry Martin (Donna Martin) and that the swarthy stout man with the flat face is her husband, Harry.

Mrs. Graham is now living in the cottage whose back garden adjoins that of the Martins.

Knowing that Mrs. Graham was moving to Mapleton, on May twenty-fifth, I succeeded in establishing myself here as an odd-job gardener, using the club manager as a helpful reference. There are not many such workers available in Mapleton, and I have been able to acquire several jobs in Mrs. Graham's part of town. Mr. Hugh Kenderton, the lawyer, has quite a large garden across the street from her, and I cut his grass once a week. Mr. Burke Patterson, the artist, on the corner beside her, was glad to turn over all his outside work to me, and I had no trouble in obtaining work from Mrs. Graham herself.

Mr. Harry Martin does his own gardening and is a fine hand with flowers; he has taken many prizes at the local flower show. He is respected in the community, if not particularly well liked. He is not exactly a man's man. He is devoted to his wife and family, "tied to his wife's apron strings" as some of the men have put it, and his whole heart and soul seem to be with her and the children. She is not liked; it is generally understood, accepted, that she is a selfish, trifling woman.

The Martins have been married for twenty-two years. They have two children, twins, aged fifteen. With them lives Mrs. Corson, Mrs. Martin's mother, a colorless, hard-working woman who has been her daughter's drudge.

Harry Martin is a manufacturer's agent. He imports and sells electrical kitchen appliances. He is not considered highly intelligent, and although he makes a fair living, he is too unimaginative—and, people say, too tied to his wife—to try new ventures which might increase his income. He is at home a great deal, never going away more than he can help. He has a branch office in Barrie which he is compelled to visit two or three times a month, but he usually manages to make the trip up and back and do his business in one day.

His father was a hotelkeeper.

Certain checks have been made on Mr. Martin's activities on specific occasions. Our men in Barrie and in Toronto are building up as far as possible a complete history of his movements during the critical months just before and at the time of Steven Graham's death. It is certainly possible that he was the man who visited the Calloran Arms just before Christmas. Today I have obtained a photograph of him which I am sending into Toronto so that it may be shown to Mrs. Cartright of that apartment building. It seems likely that Mr. Martin at one point in his career assisted in taking the census; he has held many similar jobs in the course of a somewhat sketchy career. This matter is being checked at the moment.

He is known as a man of not much in the way of temper. He has apparently given his wife a great deal of leeway in her social life and seems to bear no grudge nor to carry suspicion. But there are those who say that he is not as simple as he appears in this connection, nor so unfeeling.

One fact of importance emerges. Sometime early in January a small parcel was mailed in Mapleton addressed to Mr. Steven Graham.

The postmaster does not know who sent the parcel, nor has he any idea as to its contents. He remembers it only because it carried far too many stamps for its short trip to Toronto, and so brought itself to his attention; and because within two days Steven Graham's murder was in the papers. It was sent by ordinary parcel post, not special delivery. I suggest that this matter be investigated at the Toronto end. There was no reason to suspect that Steven Graham had received a parcel, no wrappings, no obvious contents. Did he burn the whole thing? What was it?

In regard to Harry Martin, it would seem that if he is our man he must indeed have the ability to keep his emotions deeply hidden.

Mrs. Graham is now living within his close orbit. Her coming seems to have had no effect on him. If he is actually our man, he must be living in some ferment.

He sat looking at the last line. He wrote at the end: "*He may be dangerous.*"

Jonathan Merrill had just finished reading P.C. Lake's report, on the following afternoon, when his sister Jane telephoned.

"Jon?"

"Well," Jonathan said thoughtfully, "yes. How are you?"

"Very well, dear. Getting a little bored, perhaps. Jon, I'm down street, buying lettuce and tomatoes for salad."

"That is boring?" Jonathan asked politely.

"Don't be stupid. Listen, darling...I don't know how up to date your information is. Helen has made an allowance to her mother-in-law, three hundred dollars a month. It isn't creating any wild joy around here, but at least it's something. So they're going north for the sum-mer...Mrs. G. has rented the house furnished as of next Monday, which will give her a tidy additional income, and Matthew has snaffled himself a job doing publicity for one of the bigger inns."

"Well," Jonathan said. He put out a finger and smoothed P.C. Lake's report. "That seems to be the end of something."

"We know these people through and through."

"Yes."

"So what do you want me to do now?"

He looked at the report again. "He may be danger-ous," he read.

"You might give Matthew a chance to do his sister-in-law a favor. He would almost surely like that."

"In what way?"

"She has just moved to Mapleton. Has she any help yet?"

"I see what you mean."

"Has Helen Graham ever seen you?"

"Not that I know of."

"She knows Beatrice."

"And likes her too. But...has she room for both of us?"

"Suggest yourself first to Matthew."

Jane said, "Most girls don't like working in small towns. Maybe Helen has a friend nearby who would take one of us. Would you like that?"

"It would take a load off my mind."

EIGHTEEN

Harry Martin got home from the city about four-thirty on that Friday afternoon, put his car into the garage, and then, carrying his coat, walked slowly across his back garden toward the house.

The iris, massed against the slope of the rock garden which he had built to cut the back lawn from the terraced bit nearer the house, was in full bloom, the stems were a yard tall, and the flowers were big and showy—purple and white and bronze and a queer pale gray that he hadn't often seen. It was too bad Donna didn't care more for flowers. It gave him an empty feeling inside, wanting her to care about them and always sort of waiting for her to begin.

He turned at the top of the steps he had made through the rocky slope, and looked over into Burke Patterson's yard at the opposite corner and at Mrs. Steven Graham's garden.

This new gardener of Burke's was a good fellow. He was working for Helen Graham too, and he was there now, picking up pieces of wood and nails from the back of the lot. Mrs. Graham would have quite a place someday.

She had plenty of money to do things with.

Harry move along the massed rows of the iris, his eyes not really seeing them. Having Helen Graham living there, with all her money, was bad for Donna. It wasn't as if there was any way that Donna could share in the pleasure of that money. Every hint of it hurt her, stung her. A couple of days ago a new maid had appeared at the Graham house, a trim-looking girl in a navy-blue uniform and a starched white cap and apron. Donna had never had a maid, in all the years they'd been married. Her mother had always been around to do a good deal of the work, but it wasn't the same thing. Donna had always had pictures of herself sitting in a long chair on a flagstone terrace, wearing a pretty dress, with smart interesting men and women around her and a couple of servants carrying out trays of canapés and hors d'oeuvres and pitchers of ice and tall tinkling glasses. When she read the magazines she left them lying open at pages of colored pictures of buffet suppers and fancy party foods. It was the kind of life she'd ought to have had, Donna.

She'd never been cut out for humdrum living, the only kind he could provide for her.

It didn't look as if Helen Graham had any big plans for flagstone terraces and smart parties, but you couldn't tell, yet. She had to feel her way along until she found out where she stood with people. She looked simple enough. Donna said she was plain, ordinary. She wore gingham house dresses in the morning, just like any other middle-class Mapleton housewife; she didn't even go in for country-place denims, like Betty Kenderton, Donna said. She just didn't have any style to her at all. But maybe that was all put on, Harry thought. Women were pretty smart at figuring out how to carry on campaigns.

Why had she come to Mapleton, this Helen Graham?

She wasn't simple and ordinary. Not her.

Whatever she had in mind for the future, she was filling up their lives with Graham reminders. Today Steven Graham's son was coming home.

There was this maid of hers; and the girl who'd come to work for Burke, the big fat girl that Donna made fun of, both from the Graham house. Donna had said, "She'll be running Burke's house as well as her own, having an in with the girl who's doing his work. *I* know. She certainly is sitting pretty, that Mrs. Helen Graham. Money…a new house…all the help she wants…and now Burke under her thumb. Don't try to tell me she's simple! And what's more—" She had stopped.

"What's more what, hon?" Harry had asked.

Donna's eyes, looking at him, were black and smolder-ing. "I bet she really *did* kill her husband after all," she said harshly.

Harry had patted her shoulder. "Don't say it, Donna. It isn't smart to say things like that. Remember, Hugh Kenderton's a lawyer. He catches things like that, when they get said. We're around the Kendertons a good deal… or the kids are. I'm not too sure that that kind of talk isn't libel. We wouldn't want to get sued, Donna. Best thing is to keep quiet about the whole thing."

That would scare her. Keep her quiet.

But it wouldn't keep her from thinking.

Maybe, Harry thought, the best thing in the world to do was to try to get away from here. Move Donna and the youngsters away from here, far away, to live among different people. If only he could get to some place like California! Some place bright and different, where people lived in a different way…exciting and new…

But at the thought of California Harry's heart was sick again. Take Donna to the States? Men were so free and easy there. The States was full of Steven Grahams, driving big cars, wearing sporty clothes, looking at women with freer eyes. American men weren't like Canadian men; he knew. There was a big difference. Take a woman's age… somehow, here in Canada, most women were safe enough when they got to forty. When they had kids practically grown, men stopped making passes at them. But in the States that wasn't true. A woman was a woman as long as she looked like one. They'd found out some way of taking grandchildren, even, in their stride. The men didn't count years. They even liked the older women, if they were really smart and elegant. Donna had said so a thousand times. And down there, smart elegant clothes were so much cheaper. A woman could make herself look like somebody even without money, she'd said.

And divorce—suppose a woman took a fancy to a man and he to her. Divorce was nothing. She could get a divorce for cruelty when her husband didn't take her out often enough, or didn't give her enough spending money. That's what it looked like, anyway, from here.

And what hope had he of making a go of earning a living in California? He knew who he was. He was fifty-five years old, paunchy and dull, without anything much to sell or give. It was all he could do to keep a toehold here, where everybody knew him and in a way trusted him. He always kept his word in a business deal.

Still…for his own sake, in some ways it would be good to get away. This dull bitter pain at his heart might ease up if they could get away from here and everything it reminded him of.

It didn't seem that everybody understood about pain. Donna couldn't even begin to guess, surely she couldn't, what he had felt that night when he had seen her first dancing in Steven Graham's arms. She had looked like a different woman; he had scarcely known her. Young, beautiful, laughing, gay, herself…the real Donna, the Donna he had always known existed…he had seen glimpses of her all their lives, but so infrequently. And of late years never, never just for him. But that night with Steven Graham she had come alive.

Harry put out a hand to the gray iris and touched its petals lightly. Old paunchy men with no hair weren't supposed to have hearts that could break. It wasn't fitting.

Maybe his hadn't really broken until that day when he had let himself into the little apartment in Toronto, with the key he'd had made from the one in Donna's purse. He'd known all about it, of course. He knew Donna so well; there wasn't a thought of her mind that she could hide from him. He'd had the key for nearly a month before he got up courage to use it. Then he'd been careful, making sure that Steven Graham was out of the city, out in Edmonton; and Donna home in bed with the flu. He hadn't wanted to go to the apartment, but he had to go.

Thinking of it now, of the soft shimmering pink of the curtains, the white rug, the white sofa…the bed, left tumbled, piled with its soft cushions…

He found his fingers tightened around the stem of the beautiful gray iris. It broke off in his hand.

NINETEEN

Young Jamie Graham sat at the head of his own dinner table for the first time in his nearly seven years, and was pink and starry-eyed with importance. He was not, however, insensible to the responsibilities of his position. He said to his mother judiciously, "This is very good watermelon."

"I thought it was a good one," she said seriously.

His big dark blue eyes with the fringed lashes rested on her face. "Don't you buy them already cut in two, so if they aren't very red and ripe you can see?"

His Uncle Jerry, at the side of the table, answered him. "Your mother is concerned about flies, Jamie. Cut a melon in two, and where are you? Or, rather, unless the utmost care has been exercised, where are the flies? I ask you."

Jamie turned the blue glance from his mother to his uncle, thought things over, and dug into the melon. "She doesn't want me to be sick," he said with satisfaction.

Jane brought in the coffee tray and set it on the serving table. Jamie lifted his head, swallowing his melon politely, and regarded her. He looked at her for some appreciable time before he smiled. The gap where one front tooth should have been did not mar the complete charm of his smile. He said, "Thank you for bringing me the melon. It was just what I wanted."

His mother, at her end of the table, moved abruptly. She got up and went to the serving table where the coffee was. She poured two cups of coffee, slowly, and then went back to the table, to give one to Jerry and keep one herself. She turned back to the table and her voice was serene as she said, "Is this the first melon of the season, darling?"

"Well, you see," Jamie explained, "you can't very well have melon for a hundred and forty-four boys.

That counts Decker Two, of course, and he isn't always there on account of he's been in the infirmary most of the year. He keeps getting things. So it's practically only a hundred and forty-three, and then there's always somebody missing. But you can't *get* enough melon for that many boys. At least, I guess that's it," he decided. "We get pudding."

"What kind of pudding?" his mother inquired.

He flicked a teasing glance at her. "I was just fooling, Mommy. Mostly we get prunes or oranges sliced or bananas. You 'pprove of fruit."

Jerry said, "You're too smart, kid."

Jamie stopped eating and stared at him. He turned something over in his small mind, came to a conclusion, started off on another tack, and finally said, "Was my father sick much?"

The room was still. Out in the kitchen Jane turned on the tap suddenly. She made quite a little noise for a bit. When things quieted down they had made progress. Jamie was saying, "But the thing I specially didn't like, as much as having not any garden to play in, was that you couldn't run the elevator all you wanted. As a matter of fact," he said coldly, "they wouldn't let you run it at all, if they caught you at it. So I didn't like the penthouse. I like this place a lot. Are we going to live here forever, Mommy? Is Jerry going to live here too?"

"Me, I've got work to do," Jerry said. "I'll likely hang around from time to time. But the joint is your responsibility, speaking man to man."

The front doorbell rang, and Jane went through the hall. Burke Patterson was there, big and clean-looking in a white silk shirt, his hand hooked into the collar of his big dog. He said, "Jane, will they let us in? King can't wait much longer to meet Jamie, he says."

At the table, Helen laughed. "Oh heavens, tell them to come in, Jane," she said.

The man and the dog entered. Burke at the dining-room door took his hand off King's collar. Everybody waited.

The tawny dog put his great head up and sniffed the air faintly. He stared at Jamie. His tail began to move.

Jamie laid down his spoon. His eyes were at first wildly startled. He swallowed. He pressed his lips together.

King blinked. The tail moved faster. Jamie looked at his mother.

"Jamie, this is King. He is awfully kind. His pet play-mate is a kitten about as big as his foot. If you'll just put your hand out gently you'll see what he's like. Don't be afraid, darling. He's very wise."

Jamie gulped again. He straightened his small shoulders under the white starched school shirt. He unclenched his fingers and held the hand out slowly. King moved his tail wildly. He took a step forward and then another. He brushed the edge of the table and his nose reached the boy's hand. He bent his head and pushed at it. Then he took another step and the boy and the dog looked at each other. Suddenly Jamie's arms went out and he flung them around the tremendous silky neck. He hugged King as if they were long-lost friends. He turned a shining face toward Helen. He said "Oh, Mother, is he for me? Is he really for me?"

Burke crossed the room and put a light hand on Jamie's shoulder. He said warmly, "He happens to be my dog and his name is King Patterson. But we don't at the moment have a boy in our family, so you two can make any arrangements between you that you like."

Helen said, "You may get down from the table, Jamie. And you may go outside with King and play. Don't run on our lawn, will you, dear? It's too new. Take him—"

"Take him over to my place," Burke said, "Or he'll take you."

The boy and the dog went out through the front

door. They went round to the side of the house and started across the garden together. They made a pleasant picture. Jamie's head and the dog's were exactly on a level.

Jane brought in another cup and put it on the tray. She took Helen's plate away and set the tray before her.

Helen said, "Coffee, Burke?"

He sat down. "But black, please. I'm stuffed. You know what I had for dinner? Jane, you listen too. You're responsible. You know what I had for dinner?"

Jane said comfortably, "Spaghetti and meat balls with a tomato sauce that would make anybody a fortune if they had Beatrice's recipe."

"Oh hell," he said. "Somebody told her." He looked at Helen and then at Jerry. "I don't see why we run two houses anyway," he said. "We might shove them together and save us all a lot of steps."

Jerry said levelly, "Exercise is good for people."

TWENTY

Helen stood in her living room, surveying the length of filmy curtain bunched over the end of the venetian blind. Her eyes were fixed upon it but she was not yet really seeing it. She was saying to herself unhappily, "All this is very well, but where is it getting me? Nowhere. Not anywhere."

It was very well, if you were willing to accept a superficial picture. The cottage was a charming place to live, now that she was getting it settled, and the garden was shaping up happily. Jamie loved everything and was having a glorious time. It appeared that the Kendertons across the street had a nine-year-old boy Pat, who had presented himself on the morning after Jamie's arrival and asked if Jamie might go over to his place to play. Pat Kenderton had a "super" garden, Jamie came home to report, with a brook and an outdoor fireplace and even a pool with some real live fish in it. Pat Kenderton was a happy, bright, generous child, and a better playmate for Jamie could not have been imagined. His parents must know who she, Helen, was; Hugh Kenderton was a lawyer, a Queen's Counsel at that, so he would be informed. Pat's prompt neighborliness was obviously a gesture not to be lightly turned off. It was as clear as the word "welcome" spelled out in neon over a doorway.

Every contact that she had had with Mapleton had been generous and kind, and yet people knew who she was. The Kendertons knew, Burke knew; and there had been glances, startled bits of awareness in tone and gesture from service people and delivery men that betrayed the inner knowledge. Also there had been the girl reporter from the local paper who had come brashly to the house, full of eagerness and open curiosity, to inquire why Helen had decided on Mapleton as a place to live and what she thought of it.

Helen had said, "Do you interview all newcomers like this, Miss Brackley?"

The freckled wide-mouthed girl had said, "Oh no, of course not! But…you see…you're sort of…I mean, naturally people would be interested…"

"I see," Helen had said gently. Then "Miss Brackley, could you forgo the story? You see—I have a small son. For his sake, I'd be happy not to be singled out."

The girl had flushed. She had said, "My editor told me—"

"Perhaps you could explain. It isn't going to make anybody happier to have me as a sort of freak exhibit. I'm going to *live* here. I think your editor would understand."

There was nothing to fear from Mapleton. The people were going to be kind, curious as they might be, divided as to her guilt or her innocence as they might be. They would not hurt Jamie. So why not just…forget?

Steven was dead. The past was the past. She was free and alive and this was a calm haven she had found.

No.

The past was past, but there was no future. No future for herself, and certainly none for Jamie. Someday when they least expected it, a blow would fall.

She had not yet even met Donna Martin. And when she did, what next? What could she do? What had she planned to do?

She went forward to the pile of curtain stuff on the sofa and lifted a length of it to tuck in beside the other. This was the orlon curtaining from her penthouse, gray and lovely, like smoke. She had sold or given away practically everything from the place, to get rid of old associations, of hurtful memories. But this curtain material was impersonal and she loved its coloring, and its softness against the walls. These walls were smoke gray, and when the curtains were hung the room would be gentle and lovely.

Well, what *had* she planned to do?

Had she not hoped that her coming, her settling here on Donna Martin's very doorstep, would precipitate some sort of action? But *what* action? Had she thought—how *could* she have thought—that Donna herself was the person who had killed Steven? That was not possible.

Where had she expected the identification of Donna as the woman in Steven's life to lead her? To someone else? To someone who had killed Steven because of Donna? To a man who loved her—was jealous of her? Had her thoughts been so well formulated?

It could be true. The woman had power.

Face it. She had power over Burke.

That was hard to understand. Burke seemed so open, so honest. But he would not speak of Donna Martin; it was useless to try to turn the conversation toward her. There was something between them, and it looked as if it had gone on for a long time. The paintings in his studio went back for years, for six or seven years, ever since he had come to Mapleton.

Jerry did not like Burke.

Was that not the normal jealousy of a boy for his sister, much accentuated now because Jerry was determined that she should not be hurt again? It could be that. But Jerry could never find a kind thing to say about Burke. He was too big, his dog was too big; he was too damned open, too blasted plate-glassed, too anxious to let everyone see into his house and his mind and everything about him. It wasn't natural. People weren't like that. What did he have to hide, with all that picture-window-to-my-soul stuff? There was a dark cellar underneath all that, Jerry had said a few times, until she had stopped him. A dark cellar, likely with a few moldering corpses tucked away in it.

Helen's hand, pleating the orlon between her fingers, was steady.

Jerry was jealous. And protective, and anxious.

Who were the other people around Donna Martin? Her two children, her mother, her husband were her immediate family. The children were beautiful, particularly the boy, Donald, who had obvious character. The girl needed help; she was very quickly turning into a coquette, and it was unlikely that her mother had taught her even the rudiments of morality. How could a woman so destitute of moral standards give her child anything? Perhaps she had not actually set about passing on her own tricks to the child, but children are like blotting paper. Young Dorothy already seemed to emerge out of nowhere when Jerry was at Helen's. His old car would pull up at Helen's curb and he would climb out, carrying an apple pie from his mother or a stack of his own books, if he intended to stay, and within ten minutes Dorothy would saunter past the house, and then back again; sometimes alone, more often with another girl.

They didn't look in, but Helen knew the tricks. She understood. Jerry had noticed Dorothy too.

"Who's the cute little number with the budding pulchritude?" he had inquired on occasion.

"Oh, the child around the block."

"She's on the make."

"Don't say that, Jerry. She's only a baby. Fifteen or so. She has a twin brother. They're beautiful children."

"Needs her bottom spanked, if that's all she is. Has she got a mother?"

"I haven't met the family. Well—the father. He's very fond of his youngsters."

"She'll get herself into trouble," he said darkly.

"But not with you, dear."

"But not with me, you may be sure. Not with me."

Well she *had* met Harry Martin, that first day at the country club; and she had caught sight of him, a few times since. She was planning to build a breezeway something like Burke's, opening off her kitchen—a screened room that would be a cool and fragrant place to sit on summer afternoons, sewing or reading, and a sitting room for Jane when her friends—if she had any friends—came to call; for her and Beatrice, anyway. An extra room, to be glassed in and heated in winter. Beyond it there would be a two-car garage. Walking around the house, measuring distances, she had once rounded a corner to find Harry Martin standing in his own back garden staring in her direction. He did not seem to recognize her, and although she had lifted a hand in greeting, he had turned away. On other occasions he had been in the back garden, weeding or watering or carrying out garbage, but he never spoke or recognized her presence.

As for the old mother, she seemed to be the household drudge. It was she who hung the clothes on the line and took them in again, she who went to the vegetable garden for salad vegetables, who picked the strawberries these late

June mornings. She was a shapeless, tired-looking woman, an odd mother for the exquisitely shaped Donna...or was that the answer? A hard-working, devoted, homely woman, probably adoring her beautiful daughter who was everything she herself had not been, spoiling her, truly spoiling her.

There was a tap at the front door, standing open to let the beautiful June sunshine in. Helen turned. It was Betty Kenderton who stood there, the large young woman from across the road where Jamie was playing. She was smiling warmly. She said, "May I please come in?"

"Oh, do," Helen said, dropping the orlon.

"I'm Betty Kenderton, and I'm sorry to call so soon. I know it's not supposed to be proper until you get the curtains up...but I can't wait any longer. Mostly because I've fallen in love with your baby and I had to come and tell you so."

"I'm awfully glad you did come," Helen said. "Do sit down. I'm practically in perfect order except the curtains. Tell me, is Jamie a nuisance? He's lived over there for two days now and he's having such a happy time."

"Anything but a nuisance." Betty dropped into an armchair and fanned herself. She had a lovely face, strong and thoughtful and even merry. "Pat has been needing a Jamie for a long time. All the youngsters in this end of town are much older and they patronize the poor infant practically to death. I've told my other two I'd beat them, but they are not afraid. Jamie is a godsend." She looked round the room. "This is going to be heavenly," she said. "I suppose you do it yourself. You know, I haven't got any imagination about decorating. But I know it, which is a good deal. And Hugh's sister is wonderful, so I always let her do the whole thing. I am not exactly a humble woman, but I know my limitations."

"I never did a house before. I've lived with my own parents, who have the rug they were married in, if you know what I mean, and the accumulations of years… and with my—with the Grahams, who are the same but on a much different level—and—" She stopped. Then she found herself saying, "I didn't know much about large imposing penthouses."

Looking at her, Betty Kenderton nodded suddenly. She said abruptly, "And I wanted to thank you, too, for rescuing Burke. Nobody else has ever been able to make a dent in him. Why he isn't dead of malnutrition and silicosis I don't know."

"Silicosis?"

"Well, something about dust," Betty said vaguely. "Beatrice is doing wonders with his place. I just came from there. I looked it all over. Your Jane is over there helping her right now. It's a perfectly wonderful setup and we're all grateful."

"I didn't really do anything. I sort of inherited both Jane and Beatrice."

"Well, Burke's worth some attention. He's had—" She stopped.

Helen said gently, "I've never met anybody just like him."

"No," Betty said shortly, and stopped again. "What are you going to do with all that hundred miles of curtain stuff? Do you sew too?"

"No, I'll have to find someone. Maybe Mr. Kenderton's sister could advise."

"Why don't you get Mrs. Corson? She's a wonderful seamstress. She makes the most beautiful clothes, for her own particular models, as we all know with considerable envy. She loves to sew—and she always welcomes the money."

"Where do I find her?"

"Why, she's your next-door neighbor. Behind you, I mean. She's Donna Martin's mother."

"I haven't—met Mrs. Martin."

"Well, it will have to happen," Betty said. "It can't be avoided." She got up. "We've all been through it and most of us survive. It isn't as if you—" she said, and stopped. Her face flushed. She said more gently, "I'll take you over. I sort of like her mother. I don't know why. Anyway, she's a wonderful seamstress. Come on, let's go break the ice. I was thinking of having a party for you pretty soon, and we'd have to have the Martins, so you may as well meet Donna."

TWENTY-ONE

On the way around the end of the block Betty said flatly, "I may as well tell you something about Donna Martin. She takes a good deal of knowing to understand her. She's a straight case of arrested development."

Betty was walking with her head down, her brow furrowed. "We all find her hard to take. When you discover that she's the cute little four-year-old all dressed up to sing at the Sunday-school concert, you get her number. She knows she's awfully cute and pretty. She expects everyone to tell her so, at least three times at every party. Most of us do, just to see if the system will hold. It's sort of cruel," Betty said thoughtfully. "But she hasn't caught on yet. At first the men—" She stopped.

"The men…"

"Well, most of them get taken in. They are sincere in the flattery at first. But I don't think many of them follow it up. They catch on to Donna fairly quickly. Or if they don't," Betty said grimly, "their wives soon inform them. There have been quite a few heated bedtime arguments over our exquisite little Donna."

"What does her husband think of all this?"

Betty reached out and broke a spray of flowering

mock orange from one of the bushes edging the corner garden. "Nobody knows. He's a male sphinx. Crazy about his youngsters, apparently completely wrapped up in Donna and in love with her. He never criticizes her, carries out her slightest whim, pets her and fusses over her. Her mother always did, and he always has. Nobody has ever let her find out the facts of life."

"She could be dangerous."

"She has been dangerous. I'm afraid that from time to time she may have been given too much leeway… we don't exactly know about Donna, and around here we're always on guard. But there have been tales about strangers getting bemused—and it could easily happen. I don't see how her conquests could last, but you can't tell about men. They're such kittle-cattle. She's had a few obvious triumphs. The less said about them, the better."

They reached the Martins' door. Betty rang the bell.

It was Mrs. Corson, Donna's mother, who answered the door. Her face was rather a shock. It was almost expressionless, heavy and old and yellowed, with eyes that neither smiled nor were sad. She said, "Well, come in, Mrs. Kenderton. You want to see Donna?"

"No, you," Betty said, stepping aside for Helen. "I brought your new neighbor to meet you, Mrs. Corson."

The old woman's eyes lifted to Helen's face, and there was sudden recognition in them. Recognition, and another emotion…something like panic. It was instantly gone.

"Mrs. Graham, who's bought the new cottage behind you," Betty went on, noticing nothing. "May we come and talk to you?"

"I'm making cherry jam," Mrs. Corson said.

"Well, we won't stay." Betty walked into the house obliviously. Helen followed. The old woman went ahead three or four steps into the square living room. She said, "Sit down, then, and I'll go turn off the gas."

The room had no mark of personality. Regarding its dull wallpaper, the flowered Axminster on the floor, the overstuffed sofa and two matching chairs, the begonia in its brass pot, the three magazines laid stiffly in formation on an end table beside one of the chairs, Helen found her mind going back to that other apartment which had housed the woman who lived here—the satin furniture, the white rug, the rosy orlon curtains—and thought suddenly, "There's some mistake. I've followed the wrong trail. The taste was completely different."

But there had been Steven to contend with. Had she, Helen, ever been allowed to follow her own taste? He wouldn't allow it. Had not Steven imposed his judgement, his selection, on everything in their lives? No woman would have had a chance to assert herself with him...and it might be that this woman had no real self to assert. Helen found herself listening, glancing involuntarily toward the staircase in the hall, waiting.

Mrs. Corson came back into the room. She had taken off her apron and appeared, a slightly stooped figure, in a brown chambray house dress. She looked from one to the other of her visitors. She said, "Donna's out. She's up to the store."

"But it's you we came to see," Betty reminded her. "I've been telling Mrs. Graham what a wonderful way you have with the sewing machine...and she's got some beautiful curtains to make and hang. I know you could do it for her."

Mrs. Corson shot Helen a quick nervous glance. She sat down slowly on the straight chair near the door. She said, "I don't know if I could. I'm pretty busy right now."

"You told me just yesterday you weren't," Betty said. "I know you—you just always think you can't do some new job. You're too humble. Mrs. Graham's got about a million yards of beautiful gray stuff—what is it, by the way?" she asked, looking at Helen.

"It's orlon," Helen said. "I don't know whether it's difficult to handle or not. I don't sew very much."

It was as if the old woman had been waiting to hear her voice. At the sound of it her eyes fixed themselves on Helen's face and stayed there. She relaxed a little. What on earth had she expected? Helen found herself thinking. Surely she doesn't guess—doesn't know—anything about me in regard to Donna? Surely that isn't the sort of thing a daughter would tell her mother!

Mrs. Corson looked down at her hands. "Well," she said slowly, thinking. Then, "Donna's out right now. I'd have to see—"

There were quick steps on the front porch and the door opened.

"There she is now," Donna's mother murmured, and got up quickly out of her chair. She moved forward. She said, "We've got company, Donna. Mrs. Kenderton's brought our new neighbor to see us."

It sounded like a warning. But it was too late; Donna Martin was already in the doorway, looking at her with quick fascinated eyes.

Helen met her gaze with outward calmness, but her heart was beating wildly. She was thinking suddenly of Steven in the first days of their marriage, of his dearness, his eagerness, his love for her. Of the words he had spoken to her, his wife, his assurance of love and loyalty and protection forever. No matter what happened...you are the only girl in the world for me...and his arms, so demanding, so close. She had loved Steven then, deeply and wonderfully.

So here was the other woman. One of the other women. One of the women to whom the same words had been spoken, around whom the same arms had been as close, into whose ears the same protestations of loyalty and love had been made. There was terrible humiliation in the thought; out of all the world a man chose you to be his wife. You *were* his wife, heart and soul and body. And it meant nothing to him. You meant nothing to him. You *were* nothing, you never could be again. He had made it clear. He had destroyed not only your belief in him but your belief in yourself.

Hush, Helen told herself. Hush.

Donna Martin was indeed very pretty. Her blue eyes were wide, her small pointed face strikingly pale, so that her cherry lipstick was vivid. But it was not the face, shallow and quick, that caught and held the eye; it was the body. It was a beautiful body, the full breasts held very high, the waist long and slim, the hips swelling out and then tapering gently into exquisite ankles and slender high-arched feet.

Donna smiled, a quick, brittle smile. She said, "How do you do. I didn't expect people. I guess I was surprised. Hello, Betty."

Her voice was shallow, too, and small.

Her mother said, "Mrs. Kenderton here, she brought over our new neighbor to see if I'd make her curtains. I told her I'm pretty busy these days."

Betty said calmly, "What's she busy at, Donna? Are you modeling or something? You haven't posed for Burke lately, I know."

"No, I'm not—I'm not modeling," Donna said. She pulled off her hat. "Burke's doing a special series, a lot of fishing stories. He doesn't need me for a while." She glanced at her mother. "You're not really too busy, Mother, if you want to go. I'm sure Mrs. Graham's house must be very nice. I'd like to—I'd like to see it myself." She glanced around. "You can't do anything with this horrible place. It hasn't got a thing. As I've said over and over." She sat down and fanned herself with her hat. "My, it's hot," she said brightly. She jumped up again. "How would you girls like a nice long cold drink? I'm sorry Harry isn't here, but I can do my best." She went out through the wide arch into the dining room and dropped the hat on the table. Her mother's eyes followed her. Donna went to a huge oak cabinet set against the inner wall and flung open its doors. "See, I've got absolutely everything to offer you," she said. "I'm not much good at it because I don't drink—you know I don't, Betty—but there's everything here from—well, from rum to vodka, I think. What would you like?"

Helen got up and went into the dining room, to stand beside Donna. She said, "I never saw such a liquor cabinet! It looks…fascinating."

"Harry knows a lot about liquor. His father had a big estate and used to do a lot of entertaining, I guess that's why. Me, I never drank. It's too hard on the complexion."

Betty said instantly from the other room, "It's certainly paid off, too, Donna. The fairest skin in the township, bar none."

"Well, it *is* worth it," Donna said modestly. She glanced at Helen. "Have you made up your mind?"

There were dozens of bottles of all shapes and sizes in the dark interior of the cabinet. Helen thought for a moment of getting down on her knees and rummaging through them. "A small glass of sherry, thank you."

"Well, I'll have one too," Betty said.

TWENTY-TWO

In Burke Patterson's kitchen, Jane stood on the top of the step stool and took the oddments that Beatrice handed her to put them back on the top shelf.

Beatrice was busy giving a last polish to a cracked glass bowl. "Don't know why he keeps it," she said. "But my motto always was, for goodness' sake don't throw anything away. It might be worth a million dollars. If you throw it away, sure as anything it will be."

Jane peered out of the side window as she waited. "Mrs. Kenderton went over to our house. Now she and Mrs. Graham are around the block, going into that gray house behind us. I wonder what they went over there for?"

"I wouldn't know," Beatrice said. "Isn't Mrs. Kenderton nice? So big and sort of fresh. In a nice way, of course."

Jane slammed the door of the cupboard and climbed down from the stool. "I think I'll tell you a secret," she said.

"Secret? What?"

"It's a queer one. You'll have to be mum as an oyster."

"Who've I got to talk to, even if I do talk, but to you?"

"Well, that's something, of course. Look, Bee…you remember you told me about a woman who came with Steven to the Grahams' house last summer?"

Beatrice, her eyes on Jane's face, said, "Yes."

"You remember what she looked like?"

"Yes. Just exactly." Beatrice's face got pink. "I remember."

"Well…now, I can't tell you how I found out, but I'm practically certain that she lives in Mapleton."

Beatrice's hands stopped in their work. She stared at Jane.

"And what's more important," Jane said, "you're the only person I know who has seen her and who could say just who she was."

"My goodness," Beatrice breathed. "*My goodness!*"

"I just couldn't help wondering if you'd seen her here, Bee."

"No, I haven't seen her. Although—" she stopped.

Jane said carefully, "Although what?"

"Well, now you bring her into my mind…it seems to me I saw someone the other day that looks like her. Reminded me of her. Only I can't think who it was.

I've got a picture of someone walking...and the walk making me think of that woman. Of course," Beatrice said honestly, "I was pretty shocked about that woman. I guess any other girl or woman who had that kind of wiggle to her would remind me."

"Who was this girl or woman?"

"Oh, I don't know, I can't even begin to remember. I haven't been anywhere and nobody's been here but Mrs. Kenderton, and it certainly isn't her, so it must just have been somebody going by." She looked at Jane straightly. She said, "Has she got any connection with— Mr. Steven's dying?"

"I don't know, Bee. I do know that...I'm awfully sold on Helen Graham and I'd like to help her if I could."

"Is she trying to do something that needs help?" Beatrice asked sharply.

"I'm just guessing. Only—if you do see that woman— you'll tell me?"

"I sure will," Beatrice said. "I bet Mrs. Graham *is* trying to find out...to see if she can...and she's told you...and you're helping her. Maybe that's what you were doing over at the old house all the time!"

"Don't talk about it, Bee."

"I won't. I won't say a word. And I'll watch for the woman."

Jane said, "I better get home. I'm not sure what we're having for dinner. I better go check."

She let herself out the back door and went out to the street. Young Jamie and Pat Kenderton were tearing out of the Kenderton place and coming toward her. She waited. Jamie said, "Jane, we are ackshually starving to death, and Pat's mother is out. She went to see my mother. So if we come around to the back will you give us something to eat?"

"With the greatest pleasure. What about two large chocolate milk shakes made in the blender?"

"Oh, that would be super," Jamie said.

"What's a blender?" Pat wanted to know.

"You'll see, you'll see," Jamie said, dancing. "Don't tell him, Jane. I want to show him."

"I couldn't tell him anyway. It's a thing has to be seen to be believed. Pat…" Jane said, catching the young man's attention.

He turned his red head toward her. He had a million freckles on his good-natured face. "Mhm?"

"Who lives in the square gray house over there, behind ours?"

Pat looked at it. "Oh, Don and Dorothy Martin do. They go with Elizabeth and Pete. Pete's kind of silly about Dorothy. My mother doesn't like it."

"I see. Who lives there besides Donald and Dorothy?"

"Their father and mother, of course. And their grandmother."

"Well, I know the grandmother to see her. And the father. But I haven't seen the mother. Only another girl."

"That's her," Pat said flatly. "She looks just like a girl from the back. When she and Dorothy get all dressed up alike you can't tell them apart. My mother doesn't like it."

Jane glanced at him. His mother had impressed her as being a singularly generous and sensible woman. "What doesn't she like, Pat?"

"Well, she says Mrs. Martin ought to act her age. She don't. She acts silly." Pat stopped. "She likes men," he said distantly.

The two boys tore on ahead. Jane went on into the house, thinking. She reviewed the appearance of the little Martin girl, who obviously also liked men. She was well on the way to making a nuisance of herself over the handsome young Jerry Brown, Helen's brother. Suppose you took Dorothy…dressed her as a woman…cut her hair, shaped it…Beatrice had seen Dorothy sauntering by…Was this the kind of proof Jonathan needed? It was not enough.

Helen Graham and Mrs. Kenderton were still over at the other house. Jane put milk, scoops of ice cream from the refrigerator, and chocolate syrup into the blender and made two giant-size milk shakes. She sent the boys outside with them and hooked the kitchen door. She went to the telephone and called Bee.

"Mr. Patterson's residence," Bee said, politely.

"Bee, it's Jane. Do something for me?"

"Oh, of course. Is it about—"

"Listen, sweetie. You must do exactly as I tell you. Watch out your window until you see Mrs. Graham come home. Then you must discover that you are all completely out of something—let's say, flour. Anybody could be out of flour."

"Not me. I've got a new bag."

"Well, dissimulate. Pretend. Now, you're out of flour. So you have called me, and I'm all out of flour too. Very bad of both of us. You feel terribly apologetic. So you know what you do?"

"No," Bee said, fascinated.

"Well, you go through the back garden and you knock on the door of that house behind us. And no matter who comes, you ask for Mrs. Harry Martin. Got that?"

"Well," Beatrice said, "yes. I knock on the door and ask for Mrs. Harry Martin."

"And when she comes, you apologize. Tell her you're out of flour and I'm out of flour and you need flour and could she possibly lend you a cup until tomorrow."

Beatrice said in a whisper, "Jane, is she th—is she—"

"I dunno," Jane said flatly. "But if she is, you make quick tracks right over here and tell me."

Helen Graham and Mrs. Kenderton came back from the Martin house, and Helen looked pale and tired in a way that Jane had not yet seen. She was even quieter than usual, and after Mrs. Kenderton went on across the street she climbed the stairs to her room and seemed to be lying down. Jamie and Pat had gone back to the Kendertons', the inner man well stoked with the nourishing milk shakes. Jane set about dinner, which was to be beef stew with dumplings and lots of carrots, an order from the young man of the house. She kept glancing from her kitchen window toward the Martin house. Apparently Beatrice had waited until she, too, had seen Mrs. Kenderton cross the street. But at last she appeared, freshly dressed in her white uniform, walking across Burke Patterson's back garden to the irregular row of trees dividing the block in half, and then moving through the gap into the Martins' yard.

She did not once look toward Jane's kitchen window. She went on up the Martins' back steps and knocked at the door.

It was Martin who opened it. Jane could see the outline of his bulky figure and the white of his shirt. Beatrice spoke to him, and after a moment he turned away. A woman came to the door; but from here Jane could not have told anything but that she was a woman. Beatrice gave her the empty cup.

In another moment Beatrice had turned from that other door, and, holding the cup carefully, she came out of the Martin yard. But as Jane had asked, she came directly to the Graham house. There was something in the back of Jane's mind about that bit of strategy. Maybe it was a good thing and maybe it wasn't; but if you had an enemy camp it might stir things up a little if you threw a scare into it. If it wasn't an enemy camp, it didn't matter.

Beatrice came to the door there at the corner of the house and up the two steps. Her eyes were glittering with excitement.

"Was I right?"

"I'd be willing to bet my last dollar on it. It's a different dress…but it's made sort of the same way, to show off the figure…and the way she moves her hands…oh, I think it is, Jane. I do think it is!"

Jane nodded. She began to take off her apron. "Where's Mr. Patterson?" she inquired.

"Not home yet. He went to Toronto."

"I'm coming over to telephone," Jane said. "I don't want to talk from here."

At Patterson's, she said to Beatrice soberly, "I don't want you to get mixed up in this any further, not just now. So you aren't to hear this call. And if anybody asks you anything about this cup of flour, you just be a dumb bunny, dear."

"Well, it won't be *hard*," Beatrice said pointedly.

Jane grinned at her, went into the hall, and shut the door. She got long distance and called Toronto.

Jonathan was at home.

TWENTY-THREE

Donna lay in her wide double bed beside Harry and held herself rigidly. She was frightened.

It was bad enough to have Helen Graham living there in the house behind them. It was dreadful. It had not been a nice thing at all to find her here in the house this afternoon, and for a minute or two Donna had been really panicky. But it had sounded all right, after all; it had all been Betty Kenderton's idea, about the curtains. Betty Kenderton hadn't known the Grahams before, not any of them. She had only met Helen that afternoon when she went to call because their little boys were playing together.

Everything about Helen Graham was bad, because

why was she here at all? It couldn't be Fate. Fate wasn't so smart. Fate wouldn't have led her to the only spot on earth where she could torture the very heart out of a woman, frightening her half to death. You could put it down to the fact that Burke had known Matthew. He had always known Matthew, before she, Donna, had known Steven, and lately she had been taking a kind of comfort from that. Burke knew Matthew, and Burke had a nice house in a nice suburb, and the girl wanted one too—it could be just that.

But the maid wanting to borrow the flour…even *that* wouldn't have been so bad except that Donna knew perfectly well where Burke's new housekeeper had come from. From the Grahams'. And this afternoon Betty Kenderton had mentioned it again. "Mrs. Graham here says she sort of inherited the two girls," Betty had said. "I tell her it's been darn sweet of her to see that Burke gets one of them. He certainly needed it."

Somewhere Donna had found the voice to ask whether the girls had been with the Grahams in Rosedale for very long. The one Helen had, Jane, was new. But the girl at Burke's, Beatrice, had been there for two years.

So…where had the maid been, that day last summer when Steven and she had gone to the house?

"Isn't there anybody home?" she had asked him as he put his key into the door.

"Oh, maybe a maid, somewhere around. But don't worry—my mother's maids know their place. She won't bother us. She's probably out, anyway."

It had seemed awfully rich, to go into a house where a man talked about "my mother's maids" as if they were pieces of wood. As if they weren't people, and didn't matter.

Suppose the girl had been there? Suppose that somehow she had seen them, coming or going, or—or even in the house?

Lying in the dark, Donna shivered.

Harry said sleepily, "What'sa matter, Pet?"

"Nothing. Go to sleep."

He put his hand out and patted her arm. She clenched her teeth.

"You've been restless again, this last few days," he said. "I thought you were all over it. You had such a bad time last winter but I thought you were all over it."

"Don't worry about it. I'm just—I'm just tired, that's all. I'm—fed up with this town. That's what's the matter. I wish we didn't have to live in it, so stupid. I hate it."

"Oh, now, Petty," he remonstrated. He woke up further and tried to slip his arm under her. She pulled herself away. "Don't be like that," he begged. He was silent for a little. Then, "Maybe I ought to tell you. I've had an offer, quite a while, not a very solid one but a thing I could follow up."

"What offer?"

"It's the Niffco people. I don't like them too much. But they like Canadians. They think maybe it would be smart to use a Canadian as a branch manager in their place in the States." He sounded slow, hesitating.

"In the States? Where in the States?"

"Well, right now it's North Dakota. Kind of bleak, I hear. I didn't think you'd like it."

North Dakota sounded terrible. But any place would mean getting away from here.

"How much money?"

"I haven't gone into it that far. I'd hate to leave this house and the garden and Mapleton. The kids like it so well. You don't really mean it, do you, Pet?"

"Oh, I don't know. I don't know what I mean."

"What happened today?"

"Nothing much."

"Mother said Betty Kenderton brought Mrs. Graham over."

"Well, that isn't much, is it?"

"I thought maybe you didn't like her," he said apologetically. "I thought maybe the idea of her—I mean, she seems nice enough and all, but you're sensitive— maybe you can't stand the idea of being—"

"I don't care much about living hand in glove with people who've been tried for murder. It gives me the creeps."

His hand went on patting her. He said, "Try to get some sleep, Petty. Maybe we better go away for a little trip, you and I." He turned over. He buried his face in the pillow and in about a minute he started to snore.

Donna lay quiet in the dark. But she couldn't stand it. All sorts of hideous thoughts began swirling in her mind again. That girl...suppose she could identify her? Suppose the police walked in any day and say, "Where do you come in?"

Why had she gone straight back to Helen Graham's house instead of to Burke's? Why had she insisted on seeing her, Donna, to ask for the flour? "Real polite," Harry had said. But he didn't know...

Or...did he?

Donna waited. Then she got up, noiselessly, and went into the bathroom. She couldn't go on like this. She had to sleep. And she *could* sleep. Away last fall, when she'd told Steven how hard it was for her to get to sleep sometimes, he'd had his prescription filled and he'd given her the bottle. Full. "But be careful with it," he said. "Never take more than one teaspoonful. That'll do it. Me, sometimes I repeat, but not very often. It's good stuff. One teaspoonful and you're off on a sea of dreams."

She had taken it twice; there was still most of a bottle left. Because after Steven's death she wouldn't have touched it for anything. She wouldn't go near the place where she'd hidden it, she was so sick at the thought of it.

She opened the top drawer of the three under the

bathroom shelves set into the wall. She climbed up and stood on the edge of the drawer. She could just manage. She put her hand away back, past the extra blankets stacked up there, blankets that were never used, really. It was a very safe place. She groped with her fingers into the corner where the bottle had stood.

It was gone.

Her fingers scrambled frantically into the empty space. At last she moved the blankets, slowly, carefully, one by one, and felt between the folds. She got down, locked the bathroom door, and took everything off the top shelf; every single thing. She shook every blanket out, peered again and again into the bare space, unbelieving.

She put the blankets back. Her hands were shaking. She shut the doors of the cabinet and sat on the bathroom stool, thinking. Thinking about quite a few things.

At last she unlocked the door and went back to the hall. Harry was snoring, deep and regular. Dorothy moved in her bed, and as she passed Donald's door he made a grumbling sound in his throat. She came to her mother's door. She opened it silently in the darkness and crept in.

Her mother was instantly awake. "What is it?" she said in a low voice.

"Shh," Donna said. She crept into the bed and pressed her head down on her mother's pillow. She began to shake. She couldn't stop.

"Donna, Donna," her mother said. "What is it? Tell me! Tell me!"

Donna could not speak. She was remembering so many things, things she had tried to bury. The day she had come home with the mink stole, and had told Harry and her mother that she'd bought it at a Red Cross money-making sale...for sixty dollars. Even that sounded like a lot of money, and of course Harry hadn't guessed it was mink. Fur was just fur to him. Or so she'd thought. But somehow he'd never liked her to wear it. He was always making excuses…it was too hot, or too cold, or too windy. Better wear her coat, or she didn't need a wrap…or wear that silk cape her mother had made her.

Suppose somebody had said to him, "Well, Harry, so you can afford mink nowadays, eh? Times must be looking up!" She'd thought that somebody might do that, but if they did…Harry would come to her and ask her. And she'd be surprised and excited, and say that for goodness' sakes, had some rich woman made a mistake, or had so many furs she didn't care, or had they got the things switched at the sale? She had known how she would handle that. But he'd never said a thing. Just discouraged her from wearing it.

But what was worse than the fur was the key business. Only about a month after Steven had given her the key to the dear little apartment, and she had put it on her key ring, Harry had called up to her one night when she was dressing to go somewhere, and said, "Hon, where's your purse? I'm all fresh out of money. I better go up to the service station and get some. Unless you've got lots."

"It's on the hall table," she had said. She was fixing her hair, and he knew she hated to be bothered when she was fixing her hair.

She heard him go out of the house a minute later, but that was all right. It was only when she thought about her key ring being in her purse, with the new shining little key on it, that she got a moment of panic. She had grabbed up her dressing gown and run downstairs—like a mad thing, to get the keys—but the purse was gone. The whole thing was gone.

He came back, not half an hour later. She hadn't dared be too direct. But as soon as she could she said, "What in the world did you do with my purse? I want my new lipstick!"

He had grinned. "I'm a dumb cluck," he said. "Got kind of mixed up and went out of here with it in my hand. Never looked for money until I got to the service station. Then I got some of my own. I guess I was thinking of a few other things."

The keys were there, all right. The little new key was there, and there was no reason to think Harry knew anything about it.

But there was a little hardware place up near the station where they made keys while you waited, and they were open every evening until nine o'clock.

Her mother said again, urgently. "Donna, tell me! You can't go on like this!"

Donna told her. She poured the whole thing out.

TWENTY-FOUR

Mrs. Corson got Donna quieted and back to her own bed before the bright dawn came; but she herself did not try to go to sleep again. She got up wearily when it was time to get breakfast and get the children off to school, and went downstairs. Harry came down before the youngsters. His eyes were bright and he looked rested. He said, "Donna's still sleeping. She had a little trouble getting started, last night."

He seemed exactly as usual. When the children came down he laughed and joked with them, as always, and they all went off together, Harry driving them to school on his way to town. When they were gone, Mrs. Corson tidied up the house and then finished a few odd jobs she had to take care of. She had promised to go over to Helen Graham's to sew curtains this afternoon, but there were things to be attended to first. About eleven o'clock she walked the six blocks downtown to buy some meat for dinner and do two or three small errands. When she came home, Donna was in the kitchen, sitting over a cup of coffee. Her eyes were swollen and red.

She said, "Did you get any sleep at all?"

"Enough. How do you feel?"

"Terrible. Mamma…" She started to cry again.

"Now, never you mind," her mother said. "God takes care of these things. You have to trust in God, Donna. I think things will clear up, one way or another. I don't want you should worry."

"I don't see why everything has to go wrong for me. It seems to me everything's gone all to pieces."

"Not yet, it hasn't. And it ain't really going to, I don't think," her mother said soothingly. She poured herself a cup of coffee and sat down to drink it. "I'm going over there to her house to sew on her curtains this afternoon. Maybe there'll be something said…I don't know what. I mean, maybe I can find out if she knows anything. If she don't…"

"But what about Harry?"

"You ain't really got a thing to go on, child. You're letting your imagination run right away with you. You mustn't do it, Donna. You know you get so you hardly know what you're doing, when you're upset."

"I want to get away from this place."

"Well, maybe it will work out that way." She finished her coffee. She looked narrowly at Donna. "I ought to go up and get an hour's nap," she said apologetically. "Will you be all right?"

"Oh, go on," Donna said hopelessly.

Mrs. Corson went heavily up the narrow back stairs. She didn't know what Donna might do, but it wouldn't surely be serious for an hour or so. Her eyelids ached from tiredness. She let her heavy body down on her bed and was instantly asleep.

When she got up, everything was all right. Donna had gone back to bed and was sound asleep. She washed her face in cold water, put on a clean house dress, gathered up her good shears and her tape measure, and put them into her sewing bag. She went out the back door and across the back gardens to the kitchen door of the Graham house. The girl in the uniform let her in. She had sharp eyes, that one, Mrs. Corson decided. Maybe too sharp, for the job she had.

Mrs. Graham was upstairs, the maid said, and went to get her. Mrs. Corson stood and looked around at the rooms. They were very nice. It was too bad Donna couldn't have a new house with big pretty rooms like this, big windows and new woodwork and a kind of fresh open look about everything. It might do a lot for her.

Helen Graham came downstairs. She wasn't bad-looking, Mrs. Corson decided, but she certainly wasn't pretty. You could see why a man with an eye in his head would look at Donna, look right past his wife and see Donna. This girl was tall, without much flesh on her bones, and her eyes would be kind of hard to face, if you weren't just doing what you should. Steven Graham never had been straight, it sounded as if. He must have hated those clear eyes.

Mrs. Graham said, "I'm so glad you could come. Where would you like to work, Mrs. Corson? Here is the dining-room table, I thought you might like to use it for cutting."

The material was piled on the chesterfield. Mrs. Corson asked, "What about thread?"

"I got a box downtown this morning."

Mrs. Corson glanced at her. So she'd been downtown this morning too. Probably in the Packard car Donna hated so. A body might've got a ride home. But they hadn't seen each other.

"How do you want the curtains?"

Mrs. Graham explained.

"I can go ahead all right now," Mrs. Corson said

finally, and settled into the job. It wasn't going to take up too much of her mind. She could maybe figure out a few more things about Harry and what was really going on in his thinking. But she wasn't going to miss anything that went on in this house, either.

The maid, Jane, was a quick one. She and Mrs. Graham seemed to be doing something together upstairs, and she kept going up and down. She was bringing blankets and covers down out of boxes, it looked like, and putting them out to air. They were all nice, big soft pretty blankets in pale expensive colors, and there were lots of them. If Donna could've had things like this, she'd have been happy too.

Now, take that fur stole. Her mother had known when she came home with it that it was mink, and new at that. But she hadn't let on to Donna that she knew, and Donna had gone on with that story to Harry. He looked as if he believed it, but then, Harry wasn't anybody's fool. Maybe he had known better all the time too. Maybe he had. And he'd been at the country club the night Donna had met Steven. Maybe he had seen the whole thing happening. Maybe the very first time she had met Steven in town, Harry had been watching. He might know all about the apartment. The whole story might be an open book.

What would he be planning now? What was this talk about going to North Dakota? What did it mean?

She was sewing, facing the wide arch opening into the hall, when the front door opened and the little boy came in. Jamie, his name was. He called, "Mommy!" at the top of his voice. Then he saw Mrs. Corson, sitting at the machine, and stopped dead. He stared at her.

Behind them, into the hall, padded Burke Patterson's big dog. The two of them, boy and dog, stood without moving, staring at her.

"Is that you, Jamie? Did you call, dear?"

He backed away, his eyes still fixed on Mrs. Corson's face. She stopped sewing. She said, "Hello. What's your name?"

He turned and ran out the front door again, the dog following. She saw him flying round the house. He came in at the back door and then into the hall, and she caught a glimpse as he whisked himself upstairs. She stopped sewing again, and she heard him say, "Mommy, who is that lady? I don't like her! Mommy, I don't like her!"

"Oh, Jamie, Jamie," his mother said. "She's a very nice person. She's come to make our curtains."

"She isn't going to stay, is she?"

"Shh! No, no. What do you want, dear? Don't say something to eat. You couldn't possibly want anything to eat."

"I don't really want anything. I just wanted to see you. It's lots better'n being at school! Lots of times at school I want to run and find you, but you're never there. I don't have to go back to school, do I?"

"Not boarding school, darling. You'll go to Pat's school this fall, and come home every afternoon. We'll have fun."

"And you'll always be here?"

"I certainly will. Now, could you take your small self out of this clutter of stuff and go and play?"

"Can I bring Pat over for a milk shake after that?"

"Definitely. What would you think of a banana milk shake?"

"Oh, super! I like new...smells. No...new..."

"Flavors?"

"That's it. Flavors."

"Well, we'll work out a whole brand-new set. Come home in about an hour, baby. Maybe Jane and I will have a milk shake about then too. It's an idea anyway."

Mrs. Corson sewed all afternoon. The gray curtains were going up in the dining room too, and there were a good many long, long seams to do. At three o'clock the little boys came into the kitchen for their milk shakes and Jane brought in a silver tray with one for her. Helen Graham came in too, and sat down on the sofa.

"We've been doing bedding," she said. "I had some nice pieced quilts that Mother gave me when I was married. They've never been unpacked."

"Maybe you'll have too much. This isn't such a big house."

"I think there'll have to be a couple of bedrooms over the new garage. My brother comes out often. Right now he has to sleep in Jamie's room and Jamie on a cot. I'd like to have room for my father and mother, too, when they come to visit."

Mrs. Corson thought, So you're going to settle right in, lock, stock, and barrel.

"Have you always lived in Mapleton?"

Here it comes, Mrs. Corson thought. She replied, "Not me. Harry's folks lived here. They was—well, his father was in business." She remembered suddenly that Donna had said yesterday that Harry's father had had a big estate and had to entertain a lot. Truth was, he had been in the hotel business and his entertaining had been done behind a bar. Not that it had made a heavy drinker of Harry, not by any means. Only he knew a lot about liquor, brought up in the middle of it, you might say.

"It seems a very nice town."

"We like it," Mrs. Corson agreed. She put her glass down on the tray. She went back to the sewing machine. She had no notion of doing much talking. She'd found out what she wanted to know.

TWENTY-FIVE

Burke Patterson came wandering over to Helen's about half past five, just as Mrs. Corson was going home. He put his head in at the front door, observed Helen folding material to put it away for the night, with Jane whisking around putting the card table away and dusting. He said disconsolately, "It is very lonesome over at my house and I am awfully thirsty."

"How too, too sad," Helen said cheerfully. "Would you care for a milk shake? It is now the neighborhood speciality. We have a blender. I'll make you a nice big gooey milk shake and you can take it over to the Kendertons' garden with the other little boys. Then you won't be either lonely or thirsty."

"What I had in mind," he said patiently, "was a mint julep, or something of the ilk, out in your back garden with you. Or, if you prefer, over in my back garden with me. You with me, that is."

Helen regarded him thoughtfully. He had blue paint on the end of his nose. It was a deciding factor. She said, "I don't see anything against the idea."

She went upstairs and washed her face and hands, rubbed her cologne stick over her wrists and temples, brushed her hair until it was smooth again, and put on a fresh dress of dark blue linen. She stood looking at her reflection in the mirror. She got a white handkerchief from her box and tucked it into her pocket.

Burke had carried the tray out to the table under the big multicolored umbrella and was happily mixing drinks. He had brought out half a dozen glasses instead of two. Helen said politely, "Are we having a party?"

"Practically inevitable, in Mapleton. Poke your nose out of doors with the makings, and it's like flies on a—well, let's say it's like bees on a flower," he amended. "Anyway, I invited Hugh Kenderton as I came along. Betty's in the city."

"That sounds very nice," Helen said.

He grinned at her. "Not what you're used to, I take it. It's a comfortable sort of life."

"What were you doing today?"

"Oh," he said vaguely, "a thing."

"Partly blue?"

He regarded her thoughtfully. "I suppose I didn't wash my face," he said. "I must enlarge the duties of my fat blossomy housekeeper. She can keep a pink washrag handy and catch me just as I'm going out."

"I imagine she'd enjoy it."

He sat down. He said in a low voice, "Something too good to be true about these two girls of ours."

Helen said nothing. He turned in his chair and looked at her. He said, "I have a queer feeling."

"About what?"

"I dunno, exactly. You're the center of it. Helen…your coming to Mapleton. Had you anything special in mind?"

She laughed. "What, for instance?"

"Well, I don't know. It's just—you seem to know exactly what you're doing and everything works out so pat. These two perfect servants, when servants don't exist nowadays—and you so calm, so obviously determined not to be moved—I was scared about you when you first came, but right now I defy Mapleton to do its worst, which it obviously hasn't considered, and you'd be all right. As if you—as if you were doing all this gracious-living business with your left hand and had something else in mind."

Over at the Martins', Harry drove his car into the yard and got out. He looked at them. Burke said, "Hi!" in a lazy way. Martin stopped. He turned and began walking toward them.

"Now see what I went and done," Burke muttered. "Well, the poor guy…there won't be any mint juleps waiting at home."

Martin came on, his broad face glistening a little with perspiration. He was a heavy man. He put on a wide grin and said, "This setup looks pretty tempting."

"Will you sit down, Mr. Martin?"

"Looks good to me." He dropped into one of the springy chrome chairs and leaned back. "It was hot in town," he said, and fanned himself with his straw hat. Harry gave a practiced glance at the supplies. He said, "Short of the makings, Burke? I'm always stocked up, you know."

"This is Helen's, but I've got stuff at home too," Burke muttered. He said to Helen, "Harry here is a sort of local wonder. You can't name any kind of drink that he hasn't got."

She said slowly, "I saw his cabinet yesterday."

Harry went on fanning himself. He said, "My father ran a hotel. I got a kind of early interest in different kinds of drinks. I never was satisfied until I'd tasted all the funny ones, aquavit and pernod, tequila and sake and maguey. But thank the good Lord, it was just tasting I wanted to do, or I'd have been a real soak." He lifted his glass. "Cheers," he said.

Shock fastened on Helen's mind. Then, after a moment she said, "You ought to be an authority."

He took another sip of the drink. "I guess I am, in a way."

Hugh Kenderton came round the corner of the house, his red hair tousled over his head. "I take it Burke's casual wave was a true summons to this cheery spot?"

"You're very welcome," Helen said.

He sat down with a sigh of relaxation. "Hot in town. You just back too, Harry?"

"I wasn't in town all day. Had to go up to Barrie. I have an agency up there," he explained to Helen. "It gets busy with the summer people."

There was a small screech of brakes out front and

Helen turned her head to listen. It was Jerry, all right. In a moment he came out of the kitchen door. He grinned at the sight of the group around the white table. He said, "I like parties very much."

Helen smiled at him affectionately. "It isn't exactly a party, dear. This is Hugh Kenderton, from across the street, Jerry. And Mr. Harry Martin, from the house behind you. And Burke you know."

"Burke I know," Jerry agreed levelly.

Burke gave him a quick glance and then looked away. He said thoughtfully, "The others have mint juleps, Jerry. You want the same?"

Jerry looked at Helen. "Have you got any beer?"

"Oh, no, I haven't, dear. I'm sorry."

All three of the other men rose as one. But Harry said quickly, "I live closest. I'll be back in a minute. Maybe..." He stopped and looked at Helen. She read his mind. She said, "If you'd care to bring Mrs. Martin, she's very welcome."

But he came back alone. His face had lost its ease. He set a half dozen bottles of beer down on the table and picked up his own drink, to sip it standing. "She's got a headache," he said. "She didn't sleep very well last night. And I've got to go to lodge at eight o'clock, too. I better get home. Dinner's about ready."

He finished his drink hastily and left. When he was out of hearing Hugh Kenderton said in a low voice, "I *bet* she's got a headache. Let our Donna see her husband and three other handsome gentlemen surrounding any other lady, under her very nose, you might say, and it's a wonder she wouldn't explode."

Burke sat staring into his glass. He said nothing.

TWENTY-SIX

It was in the next day's mail that the anonymous letter arrived. There seemed to be nothing of interest…three or four advertisements, the light bill, and this small cheap envelope with the odd superscription. Helen only barely glanced at it and put it aside with the others, being busy with Jamie's breakfast. But it had caught her mind, and she took it up again and looked at it quickly.

"May I go, Mommy?"

"Yes, darling," she said absently. The letter was addressed in newsprint. "Mrs. Steven Graham" had been cut from a newspaper in one piece, and beneath it "12 Sycamore Road" in another, and the word MAPLETON was in large letters as if it had come from the masthead of the local *Courier*.

She opened the envelope carefully, with the tip of her fork. She drew out the enclosure. It was a folded piece of newspaper, about eight by ten inches. Helen turned it over several times before she realized what she was seeing. Across one side a white marginal strip had been neatly pasted on it, also in words cut from the typescript of the paper, was the following legend:

DEATH IF YOU STAY IN MAPLETON
DEATH DEATH DEATH

She folded the paper together again, calmly, and slipped the thing into the envelope. She sat holding it, thinking about it, when Jane came in. Helen glanced at her, at the quick intelligent face, the sturdy look of her shoulders, but she said nothing. She got up instead and went upstairs.

She went into her own room and shut the door. She got the key to her jewel case from her purse and unlocked it. The trays swung out as she lifted the lid, and beneath

173

them, in the well of the box, was the red tequila bottle, the sheaf of canceled checks, the key to the small apartment, the empty pentobarb bottle, the letter from Milgrim's which she had found in Steven's desk. She lifted them one by one and looked them over. She put the new letter with them and locked it away. She put the key in her purse. She sat down in the low slipper chair beside her window and thought about it.

Anonymous letters can be from cranks and mean nothing, or they can be dangerous.

Did it not seem possible, even likely, that this was the work of amateurs, of some comic-book-educated youngster who had heard talk of her own past? Surely this was not the work of a realistic adult, an adult clever, adroit, enough to have murdered Steven and concealed himself with such extreme cleverness? He would never descend to such a childish trick, by which he might call himself to police attention and lay himself open to exposure of the previous crime, so apparently forgotten. She was sure, Helen decided, that not by word or deed to anyone—not to anyone, even Jerry—certainly not to Burke, to the Kendertons, the Martins, had she betrayed herself. Unless…had her interest in the Martin liquor cabinet day before yesterday been too pronounced? Surely anyone would have shown the same interest, after Donna's obvious lead.

She thought abruptly, How much further can I get alone?

She could see now exactly how the murder had been done. Exactly. Every step was clear.

But she was not yet sure who had done it. Harry Martin's open mention yesterday of tequila had stopped her dead. Unless—had he just been testing her? Had she met his test?

Above all, she thought, she did not know the relationship between Burke and Donna.

She thought again, Jonathan Merrill. He kept coming into her mind. He had done nothing for her, but she kept thinking of him, of his clear, kind, quiet eyes.

She thought abruptly, for no reason, of his sister. She had been with him on that day when Helen had seen them coming down the steps of the Psychology Building on St. George Street. It was a pity, something said in Helen's mind, it was a pity that she had not seen the girl more closely. Something nagged at her mind about Jonathan Merrill's sister. Something important.

The thought of Jonathan Merrill, who was so careful, who did not like arrests, who considered the human element first, made Helen get up again and look at the jewel case.

The anonymous letter was not dangerous. It was only a trick, a child's trick. She took a deep breath. "I'll wait a little," she told herself. "I'll wait a little."

And at nine o'clock that night, when the dusk was falling, she saw Donna Martin in a dark dress slip through the rim of trees at the back of Burke Patterson's garden, cross it, and go into the breezeway to knock on the studio door, the door so carefully closed against all intruders. She must have had a private knock. The door opened, and Helen, sitting alone in her own back garden, saw the stream of light just for a second. Donna vanished.

Was this what she had been dreading?

She put her hands over her face.

TWENTY-SEVEN

Donna closed the studio door behind her and turned to face Burke. She felt terrible. She was frightened and sick and miserable. She didn't know which way to turn or what to do.

Burke's face was black. He hadn't been painting.

175

He'd been blocking out an illustration. It wasn't the same as disturbing him when he was painting. But he said, "What in hell did you come here for?"

"Burke, don't be like this! Burke, you've got to help me. I'm—I'm practically scared to death and I haven't got a soul to turn to. Not a soul in the whole world!"

"Well, I'm in that category, Donna; how many thousand times do I have to tell you that?"

"Oh, but, Burke...we've worked together so long... I've known you so long, and you used to help me out of things. I need help terribly. I don't think a woman was ever so frightened! Burke...I've got to get away from here, I've got to. I'm terrified. I think I'll go out of my mind. I can't go through another night like—like last night...you can't even imagine what it's like! You don't know!"

"Now look," he said firmly. "Let's get this straight. What on earth are you talking about? What are you afraid of? What is this?"

"It's an awful thing. The most awful thing in the world!" The tears began pouring out of her eyes.

He straddled a chair and sat down in it, facing her. "What have you done?" he demanded bluntly.

"It's not me. I haven't done—it isn't what *I've* done."

"Then who has done what? What's happened?"

"Burke...I'll have to go back and tell you...you know last summer. You remember last summer? Last spring and summer? You—you wanted me over here all the time."

"I did fourteen poses, if that's what you mean."

"I've always been lonely. Always. So I thought—I had an idea that—you know. I used to pose for you years ago, and I always had an idea...and then, last year, when you wanted me here all the time...and you know you wanted me to pose in the nude—"

"Good God," he said bitterly. "I always want

everybody to pose in the nude. I hate clothes. But never mind. I get the idea. You're saying that you thought I was in love with you. Is that it?"

"Well, I had a right to. You seemed to care about everything I did—what I ate and wore and how I smiled and turned my head—"

"I'm a painter. You were my model."

"I didn't realize—Anyway, you got me all worked up—and then—then you didn't—"

"And then what?"

"Then somebody else came along. Burke, if you hadn't—"

"Never mind that. I'll take whatever responsibility is coming to me. I should have realized at the time that you didn't know what it was all about. I didn't understand. However, I should have. Go on. What's this other man got to do with whatever it was you went through last night?"

"Burke, this is terribly serious. Will you promise never, on your sacred honor, never to tell a soul what I've got to tell you?"

He stared at her. His eyes were steady. He said, "Why are you determined to tell me?"

"Because somebody's got to help me. I can't stand it. I can't live the way things are, I can't. Neither can—the children. I mean, it's serious. All I want is help and advice, but you must promise never to tell."

"So the kids are in it too?"

"Oh yes, yes. And I'm so frightened."

"All right," he said abruptly. "I promise. What is it?"

She pulled herself together. She clasped her hands behind her. She said shakily, "I think Harry is a murderer."

He said after a minute, "Donna, are you sure you're quite sane? Are you sure you haven't been reading crazy books, or something else that's nuts? What are you talking about?"

177

Donna moved away from the door. She went to the shabby soft chair against the wall nearest the door and dropped into it. Her eyes were burning. The lids felt as if they were edged with sharp sand. Waves of fire seemed to sweep up through her blood. She felt sick.

"Donna!"

She lifted her head. "I'm not crazy."

"Then what are you talking about? How could Harry be a murderer? Who did he murder?"

Donna lifted her head. Suddenly she felt sort of noble. If she told Burke this about Harry, she was being noble. Because he was hanging around Helen Graham, and this would clear her forever. Maybe that...maybe she shouldn't...her mind began to spin again, muddled and miserable.

"Donna, you can't come here like this, acting like something out of a cheap movie, and get away with it. If you don't tell me instantly what's back of this, I will open the door and throw you out bodily. You can lie there and cry to high heaven, for all I care. I told you last spring I wasn't having any of your nonsense, and I meant it. You act like a spoiled six-year-old who needs to be walloped, most of the time." He got up. "Now make up your mind."

"All right," she said, fixing her eyes on his face. "All right. I'll tell you. He killed Steven Graham."

That did it. Burke was as still as a piece of ice. His hand, in the air, stopped there. His eyes were blank. After a long time he dropped the hand, straightened his body, and sat down again slowly in his chair. "Now then," he said evenly, "what did you say?"

"I said...he killed Steven Graham."

"Harry? Harry Martin? Killed Steven Graham? For God's sake, he didn't know the man! Why would you get ideas like that into your head?"

"Harry didn't know Steven," Donna said miserably. "But *I* did."

Burke's eyes took that in. They went over her face, up and down, searching it. He pressed his lips together. "You mean," he said in a soft voice, "you're trying to tell me that it was Steven Graham you took up with last summer, after you got it through your head that all I wanted was to paint you? That you were carrying on with Steven Graham and Harry found out and killed him?"

"You needn't call it carrying on," Donna said. "Steven loved me."

"I see. Where did all this start?"

"At the country club. One Saturday night. At the dance."

"Steven just happened to be there?"

"You were there too. But not dancing. Everybody was there. I wore my white dress."

"Yes, you wore your white dress," he repeated. "So you wore your white dress, and Graham was there, and you started something, the two of you. And then what happened?"

"Burke, you don't make it very easy for me. After all…I'm all alone, and I can't help it if I—if men—"

He got out his cigarettes and lit one. He said after a moment, "Sorry. No, I can see that Graham could have been…I can understand that. And it was a very pretty white dress. I remember it."

Donna smoothed back her hair. "Well, that's the way it started. And then Steven used to telephone me…and send me things like perfume and pieces of jewelry…and then I met him in town once or twice. And I thought Harry didn't know, but I think now—I think now that he was watching all the time. Every minute."

"I've always wondered about our Harry," Burke agreed. "Where does he think you are right now, for instance?"

"He had to go to Toronto. He took Mr. Bates in to see somebody on business, I didn't pay any attention who. But they're gone. Anyway, Burke, it would be all right for me to come here. Harry likes you. He knows—"

"He doesn't know anything of the kind. A man like Harry, married to a woman like you, *never* knows." He got up and walked to the fireplace to throw his half-burned cigarette into it. "If Harry killed Steven Graham, I'd say that's wonderful. So he should have."

"Burke, I can't help it if—"

"No, you can't help it if. That's always been obvious. But go on, Donna. I haven't got much of the story yet. Harry wouldn't have killed Steven just because he sent you perfume and junk. What else happened?"

"Well…it's only what other men…but you see, Steven is—was—so rich. He—he gave me a mink stole, and then he—he rented an apartment. It wasn't as if I could live there—I couldn't get away from here—but we used to meet each other there. It was such a lovely little place."

"I see."

It was a relief to tell. And after all, Donna heard herself thinking, Steven Graham had been a better-looking man than Burke, and more successful, and he had lots more money. Burke would see that a better man than he was had wanted something he hadn't wanted.

"I think now Harry knew about it. I think he had a key."

"Give me details. Explain."

Donna told about the keys. She told about Harry's actions about the mink stole. She told a great many little things that had been piling up inside, hurting her and frightening her, things she hadn't even told her mother.

Burke listened. Finally he said, "Now, what has brought all this on just now? Helen Graham's coming to live here?"

"Why did she come? Why does she sit there watching all the time? What does she know? *Does* she know? Does she intend to—to open things all up, to let everybody know—"

"If husbands can find out, wives can too. I'll tell you this, Donna, as far as I know, she doesn't even suspect. She doesn't even suspect."

Donna stared at him. That was awful. Somehow… she had felt that Helen not only suspected but had probably talked it over with Burke. That he had already known something about her and Steven. What she had wanted to do…what she had thought…

"What actually happened to bring this on last night? You said you couldn't go through another night like it. What happened?"

"I just tried to find my bottle of sleeping stuff, that's all. The stuff Steven gave me."

Burke came back and sat down. He said gently, "You had a bottle of that drug? In your house?"

"Steven gave it to me last fall."

"A full bottle?"

"Yes. But I hadn't taken very much. I know now that I didn't even see the bottle after Christmas. It was dangerous stuff. There was lots of it there. Steven himself said it was dangerous. He said I wasn't to take more than a teaspoonful at a time."

"Where was it?"

"I had it hidden in the bathroom. In the highest farthest corner of the blanket cupboard. Nobody ever gets up there, not even Mother except when she's housecleaning. But it's gone. I went to get some last night because I was so worried about Helen Graham I was sick. I couldn't sleep. She sent the girl that works for you to spy on me, I know she did. It upset me terribly. So I was trying to sleep. But the bottle was gone."

"Wait a minute," Burke said. "One step at a time. We'll put Beatrice aside for the moment, if you don't mind. My brain is getting slightly addled. So this bottle was gone. You hadn't seen it since Christmas and it was nearly full. Right?"

"That's true. And Harry was watching every move I made, if he knew about the mink and the apartment and if he had the key...if he was so clever, he probably had the bottle all figured out and had found it too. Maybe he even saw me taking it into the bathroom. Seems to me I just carried it in one time with a few other things. You wouldn't think he'd be so sly, but he was, I know he was."

After a minute Burke said, "Well, now we come to the sixty-four-dollar question. How did he do it?"

"How did he do what?"

"How did Harry kill Graham?"

"I don't know. I can't imagine. I just know he did. Because—the night Steven died—that was the night I was going to stay at the apartment for the first time—Harry had to go to Barrie for the week end, some kind of sales conference. And I had a beautiful new red gown from Poirier's—it was already at the apartment. I was going up there and Steven was to come about nine o'clock. He could always get into a quarrel with Helen and tell her he was going home to Rosedale to sleep at his mother's, or anything."

"Very convenient."

"But he didn't come. I waited and waited—until long after midnight. I didn't know what to do. I telephoned his apartment once, about ten o'clock, but nobody answered. She hadn't come home yet and—and found him, I guess. He was already dead, there alone, and..."

Burke said slowly, "This opens up a whole new field of thought. Look, do you think that Harry didn't go to the sales conference, that he went to Graham's apartment instead and killed him? Is that what you think?"

"What can I think? How can I think? I just know he did. I know that I'm living with a murderer. If you'll murder once, you'll do it again. It could be that any minute he'll turn on me! How can I live in that kind of awful fear?"

"Pretty tough, all right."

"Burke, what shall I do?"

"Well, what did you hope I'd do? Have Harry arrested and stopped in Toronto, charged with the murder? Keep him from coming home?"

"You're heartless!"

"No, I'm not so heartless." He got up and paced the floor again. "Donna, now you've told me…you'll feel better. I'll be—I'll be watching, somehow. You calm down. Harry isn't going to kill you. He wouldn't hurt a hair of your head. He worships you. If he killed Graham, which I somehow doubt…" He stopped. "God," he said.

Donna took a little heart. "That's true," she said. "He does worship me, doesn't he?"

"Yes, he—does. Now, you go home and take a hot bath and some hot milk and get to sleep before Harry comes home. I'll—I'll keep this in mind."

"You promised not to tell."

"Yes, I know."

"I thought," Donna said hesitantly, "I thought maybe you might even speak to Harry. I mean…if he knew you had some suspicions, and were sort of watching—"

"Look," Burke said coldly, "there are some kinds of fools even you oughtn't to be, Donna. Come on, I'll walk you home."

TWENTY-EIGHT

Burke got up in the morning, after a pretty confused night trying to see his course. Damn it all, how much ought a promise to mean when it had been made under a kind of duress to an irresponsible fool of a selfish woman, caring about nothing really but her own safety and peace of mind? What Donna had wanted from him, what she wanted from anybody, was absolution from her own guilt. And who could give that? No human agency. The difficulty with immature people was that their own sins were too heavy for them. As long as the sins were undiscovered they were not really sins, that was the trouble. When you were completely irresponsible, as Donna was, as certain other people he had known were, you had no way of knowing what was right and what was wrong unless it caught up with you. Donna's affair with Steven had been fine as long as she wasn't found out. That was true, in her childish mind.

But if someone caught up with her, then what she had done was wrong. She still wouldn't, couldn't admit it, but she knew it. The finger was on her. God might even punish her, the awful God of the teachings of her childhood. Her mother's religion was the hard kind, completely superficial, meaningless, but tough. It held hell-fire and damnation, and Donna had been brought up on it. She hadn't talked about her own guilt, hadn't even suggested that she was aware of it, but it was there, underlying everything. She would never be able to face it. Her immaturity was too great. Her mind would break before she faced herself, break and stay broken forever. And to have to catch the faintest glimpse of what she had forced Harry to do, that was beyond possibility. It terrified her.

What, then, was his course? There was Helen.

He got himself shaved without too many cuts and went out of his bedroom. Beatrice was in the kitchen, humming away to herself. The coffee was ready.

Burke sat down at the oval table in the end of the kitchen he had planned as an eating place. The windows here came right to the floor, so that it looked practically as if the garden were growing inside. There was a stretch of forget-me-nots and pansies here along the sheltered back of the house, edging the lawn.

Beatrice came over with his coffee. Burke looked up. He grinned. He said, "Didn't I say good morning?"

"I thought your mind was on something, Mr. Patterson."

"Beatrice."

"Yes, sir?"

"Whatever you do, don't take off so many pounds that there isn't room for that dimple in your left cheek."

The dimple deepened. The girl had a lovely face. She said honestly, "If I didn't take off quite a few pounds nobody would even notice the dimple."

"Sound thinking," he said absently. "Beatrice, exactly why did you go over to Martins' day before yesterday to borrow a cup of flour?"

Her face was washed with a wave of color. She stared at him with horrified eyes.

"Come on, come clean," he said.

King got up from somewhere in the living room and came padding out. He stood beside Beatrice and put his nose on the table, looking up at her soulfully.

"Put it this way, if you want to," Burke said. "I pay your wages. You work for me. You're an honest woman. You didn't need flour. I came out and looked last night and you've got a binful and it's been full, if you don't object to the pun. We didn't get any orders delivered yesterday, I distinctly remember. So why did you go over to Martins' for flour? Are you using my establishment to carry on some nefarious pursuit of which I am not aware?"

She forgot herself completely. She sank down in the chair opposite him. She clasped her hands on the table. King moved a step closer to her. He was hungry.

"I never thought of it that way, Mr. Patterson."

"Well, I am putting ideas into your head. Why did you go?"

She said miserably, "Jane told me to."

"Jane!"

185

"She's an awful nice girl, Mr. Patterson. Anything she said—"

"What's she got up her sleeve?"

"I don't know. But I know it isn't bad."

"Is she an old friend of yours?"

"I worked with her at the Grahams'. I never heard of her before that. We had a pretty good parlormaid, Essie, we got along fine, but one day Essie just didn't come back after her day out, and her folks sent for her things and said she was sick, and then Jane turned up from the agency. I didn't know her before."

"I see," Burke said thoughtfully. "Had she known Mrs. Steven Graham previously, do you think?"

"I don't think so, Mr. Patterson. She used to ask me—" Beatrice stopped. Her mind was careful. "She used to ask me quite a few questions about Mrs. Steven when she first came. What kind of person she was, how she got along with old Mrs. Graham—she's a tartar, sir, nobody could get along with her—and all kinds of things. Then I remember she went to court on her day off—"

"Who did? Jane?"

"Yes, and she came back and said she'd seen Mrs. Steven, and that she had a lovely face. So I'm sure she didn't know her, sir."

Burke sipped at his coffee. King snuffled. Beatrice put out an absent hand and patted the soft black nose. King whined faintly.

"Be quiet, King," Burke said coldly. Then, "Why did Jane want you to go and get the flour?"

Beatrice's eyes were troubled. "She wouldn't want me to tell you, sir."

"Maybe I can guess. Maybe she wanted you to get a look at Mr. Harry Martin. A close look."

"Oh no, no," Beatrice said. "Not at *Mr.* Harry Martin, sir! Oh no."

"I see," Burke said. He got up. "I respect your loyalty,

my plump darling," he said. "I refrain from further questions. Look, I don't want any breakfast. I've got morning sickness, let us say. I am not hungry."

He went out into the cool bright morning. Over at Helen's house, young Jamie was already out, lying on his back at the side of the house, lifting one foot after the other into the air and studying it intently. Burke strolled over. He sat down on the grass. Jamie rolled over. "H'llo," he said gravely.

"H'llo. What's on the agenda for today?"

"Well, I was just thinking."

"I saw you."

"You can't see people thinking."

"I can see you thinking. You've got mirrors in your head. Two of 'em."

"You couldn't even see my head, silly."

"I could feel back in my own. What are you going to do today?"

"There's one thing. It's going to be a nice long day. I like long days."

"How can you tell?"

"Because there's no bells, and no masters, and no lessons, and nothing to break it all up in pieces, I don't like pieces of days, I like whole days."

"Me too. When I get in there painting, I don't like to feel I've only got a small piece of time, a measurable piece. I get mad if I have to feel that way. Very childish. In a nice sense, of course," Burke said judiciously.

They sat together amiably, contemplating the world.

Jamie said, "I like my mother very much."

"That's good. She seems to be rather a nice-ish person."

"I didn't like my father."

"Didn't you?"

"No. He didn't mean anything he said."

"Maybe you didn't understand him."

"That's what Mommy used to say. But I'm glad he's dead. I didn't never feel very good when he was around. Neither did Mommy."

"I bet she didn't say so."

"No, but you could tell. It's lots easier without him."

"I don't think that's a very kind thing to say, kid. It might be true, but it isn't kind. Too bad, but you have to learn the difference and make your choice, sometimes. It's what they call compromise."

"What is? Saying what isn't true?"

"Maybe just not saying what seems to be true. After all, it's only true to you that it's easier without your father. I bet it isn't true to your father—well, skip it," Burke said hastily. "My metaphysics isn't so hot this morning, anyway. You still haven't said what you're going to do today."

Jamie held out a finger and measured it carefully against a branch of the elm tree at the bottom of the garden. He got things in alignment. He said, "Well, me and Pat are going to 'speriment with what fish eat. That's one thing. I guess I don't know much more. What're you going to do?"

"Maybe I'll come over and paint you doing it. It's an idea."

"How do you paint?" Jamie inquired, frowning.

"I don't know exactly," Burke replied. "Sometimes I wonder. It isn't just a matter of dabbing the paint on. Something goes on inside. I'm not a very good painter, you know. I can make things look like things. I'm not too bad at that. But there's something that hasn't come right. I know all the tricks. I've got my technique. But I can't get through to the free place. I can't get the channel cleaned out. There's something in the way. You ought to be able to stand up there and say, open and honest, All right, God, here I go; and something would happen. If you know what I mean."

"I don't, eggzackly. But I guess you do."

"I wish I did."

Helen came out to the flagstone, in a pale pink blouse with a low round neck, and a full skirt. It was the first time he had seen her in anything but a dark semi-mourning color. She smiled and said, "What are you two small boys chattering about?"

Her face was beautiful. His answer was there. The long-delayed answer was there.

Burke got up. "God knows," he said.

She looked at him quickly. Her eyes darkened. She said, "Something has happened, Burke?"

And then, as he looked at her, the shadow came back to her face.

Burke came to a decision.

"Jamie, would you go let King out? He'll be through breakfast." And when Jamie was gone, Burke said, "Helen…Donna came over to see me last night. Some of the things she told me I promised not to mention. Some others I think are your affair. May I open up a painful subject and tell you?"

She glanced over at the Martin house and then back at her own kitchen windows. "Are you sure you want to?"

"Yes."

She walked round the corner of the house and sat down on the edge of the front porch. The front door was closed, all the windows were down.

Burke sat down beside her. "I don't like drawn curtains in my life," he said evenly. "I guess I'm falling in love with you, or maybe have been in love since I laid eyes on you. So I want to clear a few things up."

She leaned her head back against the round white pillar and closed her eyes.

"I'm not going to make any demands on you. I'm going to help. I think I know at last what you're up against, what you're trying to do. I thought I knew, but

I didn't have the right clue." He found himself groping a little, not sure where to begin. Then he realized that he'd have to go away back, because this girl didn't know him. She didn't trust him. How could she?

"Maybe I better tell you this," he said. "I don't just see the bearing, but it's such a beautiful morning…so clear and free…as if we ought not to have…well, it's like this. You see, when I was twenty I married a girl. She was eighteen. I wasn't grown up. I was all full of notions about being an artist. Not about doing the work, although I guess the right seed was there, but about being the thing. Sort of consecrated but not dedicated, if you know what I mean."

She opened her eyes and looked at him.

"The girl was young too. And…well, we made an awful mess of things. We were poor, and I asked too much of her, and she expected too much of me. To be quite honest, she was the Donna Martin type. What I was, I don't quite know. Probably pretty bad. But she had to have adulation for her beauty and all sorts of allowances made for her cuteness and her people had spoiled her. She walked out on me. With another man."

He pulled a blade of grass from the stuff beside the porch. "I was bitter. My pride was wrecked. I was a big guy, good-looking enough…I thought I was a man. But she made me feel I wasn't. I felt cheap, small, unmanly. I—well, for a while I went around proving different. It wasn't very pretty."

"Don't, Burke."

"Yes, I want to. The place where she hurt me worst," he said, and looked across to his own house, where young Jamie and King were rolling in the grass together, "she took my boy with her. He was only two. He's fourteen now. They're in California. I've not seen him since. I don't know what she's making of him. She's married again, not to the man in the case. I don't know what kind of man she married."

"That's very bad."

"I don't know that there's much I can do about it. It scared me, when I began thinking. Maybe it's made me kind of tough. Anyway…I wanted you to know what my background of thinking is. So that…maybe you'll know how I'm looking at this business of you and Donna."

"Of me and Donna?"

He put out his hand and took hers. "It's what she came to tell me last night. You see…I told you my old past. My immediate past isn't so vicious. Last spring and summer Donna was full of her tricks. She was at a loose end. She made up her mind that my interest in her was personal. It wasn't. I can't stand her. I can't bear the type, as you must see. I understand it. That's why I never paint her face. The soul shows through and I hate it. But she's been a good model for plenty of reasons…availability being one, her need of money another, the figure the first of all. I want you to know how I feel about her."

She was waiting.

"What she said last night was that I'd not taken her over, as I'd let her think I might. This is a stinking sort of conversation and I hate it, but you've got to get the motivation clear. So she…turned to Steven."

"She told you that?"

"Yes."

"Why?"

"Let's say that your coming here has frightened her. She's not very smart, but she's smart enough to guess that it wasn't accident. She's in a panic."

"Why?"

He sat thinking. Finally he said, "You couldn't open up just a bit, could you, and tell me why exactly you are here? I can't believe it's to live beside Donna, as Donna."

The red lips opened and closed again. After a long time she put her hands up suddenly and covered her face.

She sat so for a moment and then got up abruptly and went into the house. She shut the door.

Burke went on sitting on the porch. Maybe he understood. She had sat for four rotten months in a prison cell, this girl with a heart and soul of kindness and decency and warmth, locked away from beauty and truth, locked away.

How could you know what that could do, if you had never been locked inside four stone walls? If you had never sat looking at the iron bars that your own world had put around you?

TWENTY-NINE

Helen got through the day in a dream. She and Jane went through the little house in the morning and shined and polished it as it should be. They folded the comforters and blankets after their airing and put them carefully away again, but Helen scarcely knew what she was doing. It was as if away down deep inside something was beginning to break, and she was afraid.

After lunch Mrs. Corson came to work on the curtains, and she looked quite dreadful. The old woman adored Donna. It might be that after Donna had left Burke's last night she had gone home, hysterically, to her mother, and perhaps even told her part of this thing. Surely it would break a mother's heart, to know what her daughter had done, to feel the awful responsibility for what she had made her. And then to have to come here, to this house, to look at Steven Graham's widow and wonder just what part her daughter had played in her life—it must be deathly.

The two small boys were in and out of the kitchen a good deal, getting things out of the icebox to try on their fish. They had four goldfish, a dozen guppies, and some unhappy minnows, it appeared, and they were trying them on crumbs and seeds and bugs and all sorts of oddments. They wanted to make milk shakes for themselves, and Helen laid out fruit and milk and syrups and told them to go ahead. "Only don't waste things," she said. The blender whirred noisily.

About three o'clock, to her amazement, Harry Martin came knocking on her back door. He came in through the kitchen and wanted to speak to his mother-in-law. He went on through, and Helen left them alone. There was a low conversation, and he came out to the kitchen again. His face was drawn and haggard.

Helen said comfortably, "How would you like a drink, Mr. Martin? I'll make you one in this thing the boys are so crazy about. Maybe you know more about it than they do. I suppose you handle them along with your other appliances?"

He stood in front of the counter where the blender stood and regarded it thoughtfully. "No, I don't handle them yet. They're all over the States, but the duty's been too high. They're a luxury gadget."

Helen got down the rum. She broke the white of an egg into the glass container. She poured in a jigger of rum and went for a lemon. "I'll make you a drink my husband was fond of," she said.

He looked up at her quickly and then away. She turned on the motor of the blender and its loud whirring filled the room. She got a tall glass from the cupboard. She turned off the motor and filled the glass with the drink. There was some left over; she put it into a smaller glass. She handed the big one to Harry Martin and then rinsed the blender out under the tap.

"Jamie didn't finish his milk shake," she said.

Mrs. Corson came out to the kitchen. "I wanted to say, Harry, will you get some pork chops for supper," she said heavily. "And you could see if there's beet greens big enough to pull."

Helen glanced again at the dark old face. She said, "Mrs. Corson, I've just made a drink for Mr. Martin. There's just this little bit left over. Will you have it? You do look tired."

Mrs. Corson gave her a quick glance. She said, "No, thanks. I never took a drink of alcohol in my life, and it ain't much of a time to start." She stood heavily in the doorway.

"Better have it yourself," Harry Martin said. He looked a little better. "Don't waste good liquor."

Helen took up Jamie's milk shake and poured it back into the glass container of the blender. She set it in place on the motor. "He can finish that when he comes in," she said. "He's got everything in it—banana and cinnamon and cocoa—heaven only knows what it tastes like. But he's got to finish it. Don't waste good food, that's just what I said to him." She lifted the small glass of rum and poured it into Harry Martin's.

Mrs. Corson went back to the living room. Harry Martin set his glass down and said, "I better get down for that meat," and went off across the garden, a slow-moving unhappy man. Helen stood at the window and stared out after him. Queer. There was no feeling of anger in her, or revenge. Sorrow, maybe, that life could be so tangled, so bleak, so defeating.

They had dinner that night rather late, because Jamie was so busy at the Kendertons'. Burke did not appear again, and Jerry chose this night to remain in town. The house had an empty feeling. Jane went over to see Beatrice after dinner and the two of them went out, probably to a movie.

At eight o'clock Helen called Jamie in for the last time and started him to bed. She bathed him, loving the firm straight little body, going through the usual squabble over ears. She read to him and tucked him into bed with Pooh, his big Teddy bear. She went into her own room.

"Mommy?"

"You're asleep, Jamie."

"Mommy, you said I had to finish my milk shake. I didn't."

"You finished it before dinner."

"No, I didn't. I whipped it up, but I still felt kind of full. So I put it in the 'frigerator."

"Don't you still feel kind of full? You had a tremendous dinner."

"That was a long, long time ago. I would like to have my milk shake now. That was my very idea, putting it in the icebox, so I could have it now."

"Oh well, okay," Helen said, remembering that the small bones were long and not very well padded. She went downstairs and got the cold glass. It was only half full. Jamie was sitting up in bed, his cheeks pink from his bath, his eyes shining. He took the glass with such pleasure. Helen knew suddenly that it was not so much that he wanted the milk shake as that he reveled in the opportunity to have her get it for him—to be home, and loved.

"Drink it right down," she said sternly. "You are ackshually starving, remember?"

He grinned at her. He tipped back his head and poured the thick liquid down. He choked and coughed. Helen pounded him on the back.

"I didn't 'speck quite so much," he explained. "It tasted kind of funny, too."

"I should think it would. Maybe you hadn't better be so lavish with your flavorings, darling."

"What's lavish?" he muttered drowsily.

"Never mind," Helen said, and bent to kiss him.

He was asleep.

Jane came in about half past ten. Helen, sitting up in bed trying to read, heard her but did not call to her. She went back to her book, trying to make the sentences lie down on the page. They would not. She turned out her light and got up. She went over and pulled up her shade, and looked straight across into Burke's house, a hundred yards across the garden. He never pulled his blinds. He was in his living room, walking up and down. Once he lifted his hand and rubbed it through his hair in the gesture that was becoming so familiar.

There was a faint sound from Jamie's room. It came again.

Helen went to the door and opened it. Jamie was muttering. He said, "Mommy," in an odd sick little tone.

She went across the hall. He knew she had come. He said, "Mommy, I feel awful sick."

"Oh, darling," she said, and went to slip her arm under his shoulders. The light from the hall lay across him, and it seemed to her his face was white. She pulled the cord of his bed lamp. He was as pale as death and his skin was cold and clammy. As she saw, he tried to sit up and his small frame was racked by a violent retching; but nothing came up.

"Jamie, Jamie," she cried. His eyes were closed.

Jane's door opened. She came into the room in her slip. She said, "What's the matter? I heard—"

Jamie retched again. Helen whispered, "He's sick. It's not—" she patted his back. "Jamie darling—wake up!"

Jane disappeared and came back with a basin and a glass of water. Helen took the water and tried to get him to drink it, but his lips were tightly closed. The awful retching came again.

"Get the doctor," Helen said sharply.

Jane ran downstairs. Helen heard the dialing of the phone but no murmur of voices. Then she heard the front door open and it did not close again.

Jamie was like ice in her hands. He kept retching, but it was as if a tight hand was set about his little stomach. Not a drop of whatever it was that sickened him came from the tightly closed blue lips. Once he opened his eyes, saw her, and then his back arched in a horrible terrifying way.

There were footsteps somewhere, and abruptly Burke Patterson burst into the room. He looked at her and the child. He reached out and lifted Jamie from the bed. He saw the awful racking of the small body. "Jane's gone to Kendertons' to get their doctor," he said. "Go make some mustard and water. Two tablespoons of mustard, a glass of lukewarm water. Quick."

Helen flew downstairs. She found the mustard at the front of the cupboard and mixed it with shaking hands. She got back upstairs.

Burke had Jamie in the bathroom. He sat on the edge of the tub with the child across his knees. He took the glass. With his strong fingers he forced open the clenched teeth and held them. He poured a little of the stuff into Jamie's mouth. "Drink it," he said sternly. "Jamie, swallow!"

Jamie made a convulsive movement. He swallowed. Burke poured more of the mustard and water down. Jamie swallowed again. Half the glass was gone. Then Jamie retched again, and this time a flood of black horrible stuff came from his mouth. Burke got up and turned Jamie over. He held him over the open toilet. "Come on, lad," he was saying. "Come on, Jamie, that's the boy." And as soon as the flood stopped, he poured more of the mustard and water into Jamie, all of it, and held out the glass to Helen. She went downstairs and filled it again.

In fifteen minutes or so the doctor came. By this time Jamie had vomited everything that was in him. Burke was still sitting on the edge of the tub holding him, but the awfulness was done. There was a little color in Jamie's face and his hands were no longer icy. His eyes when he looked at his mother were vague but almost sensible again.

Burke said to him firmly, "You holding out anything on us, kid? You got any more apples to peddle?"

Jamie said, "I'm tired."

"I bet you are. Look, what'd you have to eat that made you so sick?"

"I didn't have anything."

"Nothing you were giving those fish? Nothing anybody let you have...old sandwiches, or something?"

"I didn't have anything, except at home." He stopped. "My milk shake tasted funny," he said, and dropped to sleep on Burke's shoulder.

The doctor came and woke him up again. He went over him carefully. He said, "He's all right now. Obviously he's got something that poisoned him. Any idea what it was?"

They were in the hall. Helen was shaking. Jane, with a flowing pink dressing gown over her black slip, looked odd. Her lipstick was bitten off.

Burke said, "What could it have been?"

"Anything. Small boys get into all sorts of things. It acted to me like arsenate of lead. Are there any of the stomach contents anywhere?"

"My God," Burke said, "I imagine I was too damned efficient. It's all gone down the toilet."

"Where would he get arsenate of lead?" Helen asked.

"Kids used to get it off old-fashioned flypaper. It isn't much used nowadays, and surely a lad like this one—still, you never can tell." He looked weary. He smoothed down his white hair. "He'll be all right now, he's in fine shape. If I were you I'd try to find even a few drops of the stomach contents and we can analyze it. Whatever it is, it's no ordinary food poisoning. He's been into something."

He went home.

Burke said, "I'll go too. But I'll be over there if you need me. Just holler out the window. I'll be listening."

He was very offhand. Helen said, "How did you know what to do?"

"As a matter of fact," he said with a grin, "I read it in a book. Mustard and water, it said, to make a kid bring up what was bothering him."

"I couldn't have got it into him, Burke."

"Comes of being a big bruiser," he said brusquely. "And he's used to men bossing him at school." He looked at Jane. "G'night, you two," he said, and went. He slammed the front door.

Helen leaned against the wall.

Jane said, "I suppose it's bedtime." She turned.

"Jane?"

"Yes, Mrs. Graham?"

"You're Jane Merrill, aren't you? I think it's time we sent for your brother."

THIRTY

Police Constable Lake walked up the path to the front door of Mrs. Helen Graham's house, and the door was opened to him by Dr. Jonathan Merrill's sister, whom he had known for some years. During the days since her arrival here at the Graham house, their attitude toward each other had been one of polite aloofness, as became strangers. Now Miss Merrill smiled in the old comfortable way as she held the door wide. P.C. Lake, having so far nothing to go on but a telephone call summoning him here, regarded her thoughtfully. She said, "It's all right, Henry. The jig's up, whatever that means. Jonathan's here and we are discovered."

"So?" Police Constable Lake muttered, his mind turning facts over quickly.

Jane Merrill ushered him into the dining room. Dr. Merrill was there, sitting across the table from Mrs. Graham. He raised his eyebrows at Henry Lake and nodded in the usual way. But Mrs. Graham was surprised as she looked up to see who had come in with Jane. She stared at P.C. Lake, who was, after all, her gardener, with blankness in her eyes. She looked pale and tired; the soft color that had begun to warm her cheeks had gone again. For the last few days she had looked younger, almost happy. Now she had got back that fine-drawn appearance. She had put on a dark dress again, too, something plain and rather severe, like a dark blue uniform, a dress with buttons down the front and a small flat collar.

Dr. Merrill said in his low voice, "This is Police Constable Lake, Mrs. Graham."

She looked at him again and smiled. She sighed faintly and relaxed in her chair. "I have been watched over, apparently," she said. "Will you sit down, Constable Lake?"

Jane Merrill sat down too, when she had got a cup of coffee for Henry Lake. There was a little silence. Dr. Merrill lit a fresh cigarette. Then he said mildly, "The child was poisoned last night, Henry."

Henry Lake's heart sank. He said slowly, "Poisoned, sir? In spite of—"

"It seems that someone tampered with something he ate or drank. Fortunately his mother became aware of his trouble very soon, and with a little staff co-operation, action was taken in time. He is recovered and, as a matter of fact, out playing already."

Henry Lake's mind was busy. He said after a moment, "I would not have expected the child to be harmed. Children…"

Jonathan Merrill's eyes met his. He said, "There is something queer in the whole picture. There seem to be too many pieces."

Henry Lake looked at him thoughtfully. He said finally, "Yes, sir."

Jonathan Merrill leaned forward. On the table in front of his plate were a number of objects: a white jewel case, two bottles, a key, a small sheaf of canceled checks, a bill that had been crumpled and carefully smoothed, a piece of newspaper with what seemed to be other scraps of newsprint pasted across it, a typed letter on a heavily embossed letterhead, an envelope. He said, "These are the items from Mrs. Graham's collection."

Henry Lake looked at them. "Yes, sir," he agreed.

Dr. Merrill ticked them off. "The key to the apartment. The checks which paid for it. The bill for the red gown. An empty sedative bottle, left in the apartment."

Henry Lake nodded. The other bottle was strange. It was red, and not large; it would hold perhaps eight ounces, in a squat full-bottomed shape with a long neck. It carried a gold and black label.

Jonathan Merrill's long forefinger touched it gently. "Mrs. Graham found this in her kitchen cupboard. The police made nothing of it."

"No, sir," Henry Lake said ruefully.

"She has handled it carefully. With luck, we shall find on it the fingerprints not only of Steven Graham but of the person who sent him the bottle on that day of his death."

Helen Graham looked at him quickly.

Henry Lake thought, I wonder what's in her mind? Harry Martin isn't too smart, but he's smart enough to wear gloves on a job like this. Then he went over again the matter of the extra stamps. That was a queer one too. Harry Martin must have been lacking in ordinary good judgement, to put four times the stamps needed on the parcel to Graham. He must send plenty of things through the mails; he must know approximately what the postage to Toronto would have been on a bottle the size of this one. If he had been so upset as to forget about stamps, perhaps he would also have forgotten about fingerprints...

He looked intently at Dr. Merrill, who was smoking thoughtfully.

Jane Merrill got up from the table and went to the kitchen, to stand and look from the window toward the Martin house. She said, "The children and their father are on the back porch. They're coming out the door… he's about to drive them to school. He's got his suit coat on and his raincoat over his arm. He's going to the city."

Dr. Merrill said to Mrs. Graham, "Mrs. Corson is coming here to sew?"

"I asked her if she could manage it fairly early so we could finish the curtains today. She thought she could come at nine."

"Is there any way to get Mrs. Martin out of her house?"

Helen Graham looked at Jonathan Merrill. "Burke Patterson could get Mrs. Martin out of the house. She loves to pose for him."

"Will you call Mr. Patterson?" Dr. Merrill asked.

She got up and went to the telephone in the hall.

Dr. Merrill said, "I have a search warrant, Henry."

Henry Lake nodded. He was marshaling his facts. There would be a number of things to look for—four or five items, anyway. Perhaps something unforeseen would be discovered as well.

Mrs. Graham came back. "He's glad to do it," she said. Her cheek wore a faint flush again, and her eyes were not quite so brooding. Burke Patterson was good for her, Henry Lake told himself. He was a big, openhearted, sincere man, not like the twisted, contriving creature that Steven Graham had been.

The clock struck nine.

Jonathan Merrill got up from the table. His careful hands set the array of items back into the white jewel case. He handed it to Jane.

There was a knock at the back door. Mrs. Graham said under her breath, "Mrs. Corson."

Jane Merrill whisked into the living room with the white box. Jonathan Merrill moved toward the front door.

"There's a car waiting down at the corner," he murmured to Henry Lake, and they went on out together.

Mrs. Corson came in heavily, her shoulders stooped and tired. She glanced round the dining room quickly as she came in, but the sight of extra cups on the table apparently meant nothing to her. Helen said, "Good morning, Mrs. Corson," and set about clearing the table.

The old woman dropped down on the edge of a chair, waiting. Her face was gray, her eyes dull. Helen said, "You look tired."

"Yes," Mrs. Corson said in a lackluster voice. "I didn't get much sleep. I don't always sleep very well." She glanced up quickly. "You folks all feeling fine today?"

It was as if a small finger touched warningly at Helen's heart. She heard herself answering slowly, "Why, yes, thank you. That is—Jamie had a little upset in the night, but he's all over it. He's—he was pretty sick. But he's all right."

"Well, that's good," Mrs. Corson said. The intent eyes dropped. She muttered, "Maybe the water here don't agree with him."

"It seems to agree with other children," Helen said. "Your two are certainly healthy, and so is Pat and the other two Kendertons."

Mrs. Corson nodded. Her hands clutched firmly at her sewing bag. It was as if her mind were turning something over, as if she had something she wanted to say but could not quite bring herself to it.

Helen finished clearing the table. She got the portable Singer and set it on the table. She plugged in the cord and got a chair in position. Mrs. Corson, watching her, got up silently. She took the roll of curtain material from the sideboard and spread it out on the table. But when it lay there she stood looking down at it as if she did not see it. Once she reached up and twisted a strand of her thin hair back into place, so that it lay neatly along her skull and was caught into the small knot at the back.

Through the window, Helen caught sight of Donna Martin, running across the corner of Burke Patterson's garden. At the same moment the police car which had been sitting down at the corner started up and swung round into the side street.

Mrs. Corson took a long breath and unrolled her material. She settled down to her sewing.

An hour or more went by. The house was quiet, save for the whir of the small machine. Jane was busy in the kitchen. Helen went upstairs and made beds. She came down and dusted the living room. Her throat ached, and her hands fumbled. She didn't know what she wanted or didn't want, or what she thought or didn't think.

The front door bell rang. Jane answered it. Her brother entered, followed by Police Constable Lake, who carried a parcel. It looked like a big roll of newspapers. Something blue was around them.

The men stopped in the hallway and Helen went out to them. Jane was at the foot of the stairs. Mrs. Corson's machine stopped for a moment and she looked up. Her eyes fell on the roll of papers. She stared at them.

She got up from her chair. Her eyes were no longer dull; they blazed. She said in a thick voice, "Where'd you get them papers? They're mine! That's the roll I had tied with Dorothy's blue—" She stopped.

"Yes," Jonathan Merrill said quietly.

"What right have you got to go to our house and get into my room? Who are you? What's going on here, anyway?" She looked about wildly. "Where's Donna? What've you done with Donna?" She moved out from behind the table. "I've got to go home. Where's Donna? I want to know what goes on here."

Helen said gently, "She's over at Burke Patterson's, Mrs. Corson. You know that. He called her to come over and pose."

She said bitterly, "I don't believe it. You got her out of the house—you've done something to her...I knew the minute you come here, it wasn't good. You're all against her and she never had a chance. What did you come here for, spoiling everything? I want Donna! What've you done with her?"

There were heavy footsteps on the front walk, and two policemen in blue uniforms came unceremoniously into the house through the open door. Between them was Harry Martin.

He looked at Helen and then at his mother-in-law, at Jane and Jonathan and Constable Lake. His eyes were utterly bewildered. He said, "I don't know what in God's name this is all about, but I demand an explanation. I'm a citizen and I've been stopped like a common criminal and dragged back here—Mother, what are they doing to you? Where's Donna? What is this, anyway?"

THIRTY-ONE

Someone had gone for Burke and Donna. Helen, standing at the end of the room, her fingers cold on the back of the chair she held to, looked at the people in her quiet living room with sick eyes. Harry Martin, beside his mother-in-law, was patting her shoulder awkwardly and apparently trying to question her and quiet her at the same time. She kept wringing her hands and speaking of Donna, not making any sense to Harry. But something of her fear, her terror for Donna, got through to him at last. He turned to Jonathan Merrill and said, "See here, you seem to be the boss around here. I don't get this at all. My wife's missing, my house has been searched, my mother-in-law here is out of her mind with worry about something, and I've been arrested. I don't know what this is all about, but I know my rights.

I'm a citizen. These policemen can't do this kind of thing to a citizen. I demand a lawyer."

Jonathan did not answer. Harry said again, "You heard me! Send one of these men for Hugh Kenderton, across the street. He hasn't left for town yet, he never leaves until ten o'clock. Get him. I demand a lawyer."

Jonathan said gravely, "You are at liberty to telephone him, Mr. Martin. You are quite within your rights in having him here."

Harry looked about him wildly. Jane moved in from the doorway and touched his arm. She rang Central for him. He gave a number, loudly. He waited a moment, then said, "Hugh? Harry Martin. Look, for God's sake— get over to Mrs. Grahams right away, will you? I don't know what's going on—I was stopped on the highway and brought back by a couple of policemen. Donna seems to be missing and her mother's—No. No. Yes. Now. Yes." He hung up. He said to the room at large, "Now, what has happened to my wife? What is the trouble?"

P.C. Lake, with Donna and Burke in front of him, appeared at the open door. Donna came in first, her hands pressed over her mouth, her eyes wide, staring, blank with terror.

Harry turned and saw her. He took a step forward and put his arms around her. He said, "Where were you? What happened? Are you hurt? What did they do to you? Donna, Donna, are you all right?"

She pulled back violently from his arms and shuddered visibly. She turned toward Burke, but he caught her arm and pushed her forward into the room. "Sit down," he said coldly.

Harry's face went gray. He said under his breath, "What's happened to her? Why is she acting like that to me?"

Hugh Kenderton came running across the front lawn. He took two steps up to the porch and into the house. He looked around with startled eyes at the policemen, at Donna sitting in her chair with her hands pressed to her face, at old Mrs. Corson staring straight ahead of her as if she were paralyzed. He looked at Harry, whose whole attention was fixed on Donna. His eyes went past Harry to Helen, standing alone at the end of the room, and came at last to Jonathan Merrill, who had put his roll of newspaper down on the desk on the side wall and who had been saying a word or two to P.C. Lake. Hugh Kenderton said, "Well, Jon Merrill! Thank God, here's a little hope for some sense. What on earth is all this schemozzle? What kind of trouble is Harry in, and all his family?"

Jonathan Merrill looked at him and nodded in his preoccupied way. "It isn't a very long story, Hugh." The room fell silent. Everyone was looking at him but P.C. Lake, who had got Helen's jewel case and opened it, there on the desk. He took out of it the things she had collected and put them with the roll of paper on the desk, the roll tied with the blue cloth. He untied the knot in the blue cloth. Mrs. Corson, watching him made a convulsive movement.

Jonathan said, "Henry, will you state the facts."

P.C. Lake flicked him a glance, but stood up.

From his place near the door Burke said, "This gentleman, to the best of *my* knowledge, is my gardener. Am I mistaken?"

Jonathan said, "Police Constable Lake, Mr. Patterson. He has been here collecting certain information needed to clear up the death—still unexplained, you may remember—of Steven Graham, which took place on the seventh of January last."

Hugh Kenderton said quietly, "Just a minute. I should like to remind my client, Mr. Martin, that he is not required to answer any questions or to commit himself in any way at this point."

Harry Martin stared at him. He said, "Thanks, Hugh. But—I'm completely in the dark. I haven't—I don't—" He stopped.

P.C. Lake coughed. He said evenly, "I will attempt to relate this story in order."

The room quieted again.

"Last August," P.C. Lake said steadily, "Mr. Steven Graham visited the Mapleton Country Club on a Saturday night, at which time he met Mrs. Harry Martin. The meeting was the beginning of a series of meetings."

Donna Martin gasped. She stared up at Burke wildly.

"One of the meetings was in the same month, at the house of Mrs. Graham, Sr., in Rosedale," P.C. Lake went on inexorably. "At that time Mrs. Martin was seen, and has been since identified, by Beatrice Greene, at that time cook for the Grahams and now employed by Mr. Burke Patterson as his housekeeper.

"On the first of November, Mr. Steven Graham rented an apartment at number 10 Calloran Street. During the next two weeks he made various purchases of furnishings for the apartment. The lock was changed. Mr. Graham gave one key to Mrs. Martin and retained the other for his own use."

Hugh Kenderton glanced quickly at Helen. He walked across the room and found a chair. He sat down slowly. He listened.

"On the fourteenth of November," the calm voice went on, "Mrs. Martin made the purchase of a mink scarf, or stole, in Poirier's for which she paid seven hundred dollars in cash. She wore the stole several times in Mapleton, which caused some comment among the ladies of the town, who knew its value.

"On an evening late in November," P.C. Lake said carefully, "Mr. Harry Martin took a small new Yale key to the key makers here in Mapleton, Gorgias and Smith's, and had a copy made."

Harry Martin took a slow step backward. He set his heavy shoulders against the wall.

"About the middle of December, Mr. Martin paid a visit to the apartment at number 10 Calloran, and was seen coming out of the apartment rented by Mr. Graham under the name of H. Brown, his wife's maiden name. A photograph of Mr. Martin, obtained from the local photographer here, has been identified by the caretaker of the apartment as the man she saw on that occasion."

Martin said heavily, "This is—I didn't—it isn't—" He stopped.

P.C. Lake said, "On the sixth of January a small parcel, about ten inches long by four inches square, was mailed in the Mapleton post office to Mr. Steven Graham. It is remembered because it had been given nearly a dollar's worth of stamps, four times too many for its trip to Toronto. The postmaster, noticing this, remembered the parcel when the news came out.

"On the next day, January seventh, Steven Graham was found dead in his apartment of an overdose of elixir of pentobarbital, a sleeping drug he made free use of. Because of motive, opportunity, and a piece of apparently strong evidence produced against her, Mrs. Steven Graham was arrested on suspicion of the murder. After nearly four months in prison she was tried at the spring assizes, and because of insufficient proof of guilt, she was acquitted."

Kenderton got up. He looked at Helen unhappily. He said, "It becomes clear why Mrs. Graham chose this neighborhood to move into."

Donna began to sob. Her mother looked at her miserably.

"It was the opinion of Dr. Merrill, who had been early called in on the case," P.C. Lake went on, "that Mrs. Graham was not only innocent but that she might possess information which would eventually lead her—and the police, if she were properly observed—to the true killer."

Kenderton said, "How was it done, Jon?"

Jonathan Merrill said soberly, "It appears that what was in the parcel received by Steven Graham was a bottle of liquor, unfamiliar, whose taste he was unlikely to know. It seems probable that the liquor was heavily dosed with the drug." He glanced at P.C. Lake.

Kenderton said, "Not everyone has access to that drug."

Constable Lake unrolled the bundle of newspapers on the desk. A number of things were inside. He took up one; it was a bottle, empty, an eight-ounce medicine bottle with a blue label. "This was found half an hour ago in the Martin house," he said. "It is considered likely that Steven Graham gave it full to Mrs. Martin, since it bears his name and prescription number. He would scarcely give it to her empty. We take it that a quantity of the drug, therefore, was in the Martin house at the necessary time."

Donna said to Burke wildly, "You viper—you liar, you devil—you did this! You told!"

"Matter of fact, I didn't," Burke said levelly.

Harry said to her roughly, "Be quiet."

Mrs. Corson sat like a stone image.

P.C. Lake lifted the dark red glass bottle with its distinctive label. "This bottle was found by Mrs. Graham in her own cupboard, it having been put there sometime between four o'clock on the afternoon of her husband's death, when she left the apartment, and eleven that night, when she saw it. It is our present belief that he drank the liquor in the bottle, and then, as was his custom, washed his glass and put it and the bottle away. The bottle has not yet been tested for prints. It is unlikely that those of the criminal will appear since the most inexperienced criminal nowadays knows enough to wear gloves. However, we may be fortunate."

Harry Martin said in a harsh voice, "That bottle will have my fingerprints. I don't know how it got out of my house, but it came from my—" he stopped. "My God, what have I said," he groaned.

"On the search conducted in Mr. Martin's house this morning," P.C. Lake went on, "we discovered in his liquor cabinet twenty-three further bottles in varying colors and with different labels, containing the specialty liquors of various countries." He held up a green bottle, a yellow one, one of amber. They were identical in shape and size with the tequila bottle. "Mrs. Graham found in Mr. Graham's desk a letter from a leading distiller suggesting that he was sending a sample of a new type of product. The letter began 'Dear Sir'; it was dated almost a year before Steven Graham's death. It seems that the letter had been sent to Mr. Harry Martin with the consignment of interesting foreign liquor samples, a year previously, and was never meant for Steven Graham."

There was a hush in the room. Hugh Kenderton got up and walked a pace or two up and down the room. He sat down again. He said, "You are disclosing all your evidence very freely. May I inquire how it was possible for Steven Graham to take a lethal dose of the drug and then wash his glass and put the bottle away? The bottle you hold would seem to be capable of containing at least eight ounces of liquid. At least half of that, if the dose was to kill him, must have been the straight undiluted drug. I realise that since it was rendered tasteless in preparation he might not have noticed it in an unfamiliar liquor, particularly one such as tequila. But he would surely have had to drink it very quickly...and then can you prove that it was sufficient to kill him?"

Police Constable Lake stood silent. Jonathan Merrill said, "We do not think that the drug in the tequila did kill Steven Graham." He leaned forward. He said, "Mrs. Corson, do you hear that? We do not believe that you murdered Steven Graham."

THIRTY-TWO

Jonathan Merrill repeated, "Mrs. Corson...did you hear what I said? They won't be able to prove that you killed Steven Graham, after all."

The room was absolutely silent. Helen was stunned with surprise; Donna's face, staring at her mother, was blank, uncomprehending. Kenderton, Harry Martin, Burke...they stared at Jonathan Merrill.

Mrs. Corson moved. Her voice was hoarse. She said, "I never killed anybody in my life. I never really meant to."

"You almost killed Jamie, last night, with the stuff you soaked off the flypaper."

She said dully, "But he didn't die. It was the same thing. I put it all in God's hands. I just wanted to scare her. I told God that. He knew. If He didn't want the boy to die, He'd save him. I prayed hard to God to just scare her away. We couldn't live no longer with her here. Donna would go crazy. She couldn't stand no more."

"When you sent the tequila to Steven Graham did you pray?"

"Yes, I did. It was his own stuff I sent him. He shouldn't have been taking it. He shouldn't have drunk liquor all the time, the way he did. I knew all about him; Donna told me the whole thing. I was worried. I was just sick, worrying. But when I sent it I knew it wouldn't kill him if God didn't intend him to die. I didn't know how much to use, but I didn't figger it made any difference. It was up to God. He needed a little help right then to make the man do what was right. What I thought—maybe he would just go sound asleep and never go to the apartment at all. I didn't rightly mean to kill him; I knew God would take over." She looked at Jonathan steadily. "Did he take some more, himself?" she asked. "Is that why I didn't do it? Why I'm not to blame?"

"I didn't say you weren't to blame," Jonathan said. "I said, you didn't kill him. Yes, we think he took more. But he'd drunk yours first. It's a legal point. The lawyers can battle over it. But about Jamie—and this letter—we found the scraps of newspaper in your room. You pasted it and sent it to Mrs. Graham—"

"Why did she come here?" the old woman said pitifully. "Why did she have to come here? We couldn't stand it no longer, we couldn't. She had to go away."

Jonathan nodded. He got up. "Hugh. You want to do anything about this?"

Hugh Kenderton said quietly, "My God and little apples, Harry—"

Harry looked at him. His face sagged. He shook his head hopelessly. "I don't think she meant any real harm," he said. "It's just—you know, we couldn't—she's right. I guess we couldn't've stood much more."

Donna flung herself off the chair. She turned toward Helen. Her face was wild with fury. She spat her words out. She said, "Look what you've done, you she-devil! Look what you've done now, ruining my life, breaking up my whole life! Look what you've made my mother do, coming here standing over us all like a—like—"

Burke, standing behind her, clapped a hard hand over her mouth. He slid an arm under her and carried her bodily out of the house. At the doorway he turned to Harry. "What do you want done with this piece of worthless baggage?" he inquired. "Come and get it if you want it, or I'll drive straight to the town dump and throw it on."

THIRTY-THREE

It was late evening. In her quiet living room, Helen sat alone. Jane was still in Mapleton, having refused to go back to the city with her brother. "He'll need me soon enough," she had said comfortably, when Helen had taken for granted that she was going. "Next case I'll have to dig ditches or maybe hunt down great masses of information out of the encyclopedia, or sit for interminable hours in the hospital listening to the ravings of some disturbed patient suspected of something or other. He doesn't need me now. I won't go back to Toronto for a few days—until you find someone to come and live with you."

She was a dear little girl, Helen had thought. Jerry, arriving in late afternoon after a call from Helen, had seemed to think so too. They were about of an age, Jane and Jerry, although her years of sober responsibility in working with Jonathan had made her appear older.

They had gone for a drive, at Helen's insistence. "I want to be alone," she had said. "I want to get my mind straight about things."

She walked now to the window at the back of the house and stared out toward the Martin dwelling. Donna and Harry were there. They had come back from Toronto, but Mrs. Corson was not with them. Helen knew where the old woman was; she could remember the smell of the dirty old prison, the echoing footsteps on the bare floors, the rustling miserable sounds of the other prisoners behind their steel bars. What would happen to her? She would not be acquitted, she would never be set free. Her lawyers, as Jonathan pointed out, might be able to get her off the murder charge on a technicality, but she had confessed to sending the drug to Steven, to putting poison in Jamie's milk shake. There would be a serious charge against her and she would live out her unhappy days in prison.

There would be a wave of tremendous publicity. It would break tomorrow. It had to break; nothing but publicity could free Jamie. Nothing but the most complete airing of the truth.

Over there in the Martin house...Donna and Harry, facing each other at last, with their two beautiful children asleep upstairs; what was to become of them? Another place to live, somewhere far away...a new life for them all. For the children, life might be bearable after a time. Never for Donna, not for Harry, loving her. Her mind would probably break, Jonathan had suggested. She had not been taught to take or carry personal responsibility; she could not begin now.

Helen went back to her chair and picked up her knitting. She was doing a pair of socks for Jamie; just socks, plain and straight ahead. A pattern would have been beyond her powers of concentration.

Jamie was happy, and now he could stay happy. At dinnertime he had come in with Burke, spattered and smeared with paint, carrying carefully a miraculous painting. He had been so proud of it. There was a bright yellow sun exactly in the middle of the canvas, and some fairly obvious trees in a neat row all around the edge. One tawny lump with four projections was obviously King. One round object with a white skirt appeared to be Beatrice.

"Why, it's wonderful, Jamie," Helen had said warmly, loving the smiling little face.

"It has a very, very speshul name," Jamie told her importantly.

"Has it now?"

Burke said carefully, "It's a primitive. A very neat little primitive. It isn't everyone who could turn out a primitive at the very first go."

"See?" Jamie said. "See what I did?" He went across to Jerry. He said, "Could you do a primitive if you tried?"

Jerry, deeply if silently appreciative of what Burke had last night done for his small nephew, put a swift arm around the boy and gave him a quick hug. He said gruffly, "I guess I could do almost anything I tried, except paint a primitive."

Now Jamie was asleep, and safe, upstairs. They had their little house, and they had a clean record, she and Jamie.

Or…had they?

She was sitting there in the quiet when there was a knock at the front door and it opened. Burke came in. He stood in the doorway, almost as tall as the top of the door. He was wearing a blue sweater and old gray trousers.

"May I come in?"

"With pleasure," Helen said, and put down her knitting.

"I like to see you doing that."

"I've just dropped three stitches."

He sat down in the armchair near the door. He locked his hands under his chin and stared at her over them. He said, "You're not really beautiful. But you're extremely satisfying to look at."

"That's something."

"You'll probably never be fat."

"I hope not."

"How old are you?"

"Twenty-eight." She smiled at him. "Is that all right?"

He said, "Do you still love your husband at all? I don't see how you could, but women are funny about love."

"I don't think I ever loved him. Not enough. I've been sitting here with the most awful sense of failure."

"Failure?"

She put a hand to her brow and looked at him from beneath it. "I have to keep pushing down my thinking.

This thing looks cleared up, in a way, but it isn't. The clearing up is only superficial."

"I don't think I know what you mean, my dear."

The words touched her. "Well, it's this way…Steven wasn't to blame for what he was. You may say he was his mother's fault. But what made her what she was? A soured, embittered woman…full of fears and pretense. Why was she so?"

"Life does bad things to people."

"That isn't good enough, Burke. There has to be an answer somewhere instead of just the continuing of a problem. Suppose you do start with Mrs. Graham—no, her father. Her father was a drunkard, I don't suppose you know that. He was a terrible man—they were fairly well to do, but he used to come home and beat her mother, and she knew. She married to get away from that sort of living…and her own husband, who had appeared to be so fine, turned out to be loose. You may say…her attitude did that to him. I think it did. But her attitude wasn't her fault. It was forced upon her. So she wrecked her husband…and her sons. But it wasn't her fault. Do you see?"

"Dimly."

"And then…Steven turned to me for help."

"What do you mean there?"

"Oh, don't you see?" Helen cried. "I was different, Burke! He wanted me, he married me, because I wasn't like his mother. For once in his life Steven tried to break his pattern. He turned to me for help. I hadn't any of the stigma in my life that had marked him. My people are so ordinary, so simple. They don't drink, they go to church and they teach and work hard and do what's right. They have a very simple set of moral standards and they adhere to them; they're honest and clean-living and they try to treat their neighbors as themselves. That's what Steven wanted when he turned to me." She felt the tears coming up behind her eyes. "Understanding sympathy, *true* sympathy. Help to be his better self. He didn't get it," she whispered. "I failed him."

Burke got up and began to pace the floor. He looked down at her once or twice and then went back to his chair. He said quietly, "What could you have done? Weren't you the product of your environment too?"

"Yes, I know. Rather prudish, narrow-minded, inflexible…not too tolerant. I can see it now. If only—if only I'd understood what he needed—help to change, to be free of his own past—and if I'd truly loved him, Burke, I could have saved all this. All this misery and horror. Mrs. Corson, only trying to protect her child, to save her from evil, to save her from herself…Donna, so weak and helpless, such a baby, spoiled and immature and helpless. It was in my hands to save us all. And I didn't do it."

The clock on the mantel ticked loudly in the stillness. Burke sat looking at her with eyes that were shadowed, full of understanding, full of pain. "I know what you mean," he said gruffly. "I did it too, Helen. If I'd understood—if I'd been big enough—my wife wouldn't have had to go somewhere else for whatever it was she needed. Maybe she wasn't bad. Maybe nobody is. Just lonely and lost, in need of something…and we look at each other and don't see the need, don't try to fill it. So people run away in some kind of desperation."

Helen wiped his eyes with her knitting. "You do see. I'm terribly grateful, Burke."

"I want to go and find my boy and try to—to make up for what I haven't been to him." He looked at his big hands. "That sound sentimental to you?"

"It sounds like the only sense there is. When we've failed, and know it…I guess it's just further weakness to keep on weeping. The thing to do is to try and restore what is lost. I'm—I guess I'll go to Mrs. Graham and tell her how I failed Steven. I guess I will. And of course she must have money, if that's what she needs and wants. Heaven knows it isn't my money, anyway, and why should I set myself up as judge, jury, and executioner? As for Donna…and Harry…and those children…" She found an old blackness welling up in her. "I haven't got the generosity to say I ought to help them too. She—she broke my self-respect into little pieces. When your husband finds another woman so much better than you are…it does something terrible to your pride. Maybe I can handle that one sooner or later. I don't know. Right now—"

"Don't go too fast," Burke said. "You'll get up on a cloud somewhere and leave me down below. Helen… you're going to marry me, aren't you? I need you very much. I suppose it's too soon to think about it. I'm in love with you, but it's too soon…do you know how I feel, when I'm in love with you?"

"No," Helen said slowly. "I don't know about men. Steven was never honest with me. In some ways I am extremely ignorant."

Burke said warmly, "Well, that's marvelous. Do you want I should try to get it across?"

Their eyes met and held. His were anxious, loving, hopeful. He said, "It seems such a waste of time, living like this, when you're so near."

She said, "Jerry says I'm frozen in a block of ice. I think it's true. But—your honesty, Burke—I love it. The freezing is only defense against falseness. And, if you know what I mean—my own falseness as much as anyone else's. So will you give me time to find myself?" She smiled. "And then you can help my boy to be a neat little primitive…and I'll go with you to find your son. But you know what I have to do first, somehow?"

"What?" Burke said. "Something tough?"

"Very tough," Helen said. "I have to get my sense of

humor out and polished up. I have to learn to laugh, mostly at me."

Burke grinned. He said happily, "I think I will teach you to be a neat little primitive too."

Helen said, "I guess that's what they all were. Back in the Garden, before any of this trouble began. I guess that's it. Neat little primitives."